─────── ★ ───────

"BUT THE BOY HAS GOT TO BE *SOMEWHERE*," HOOKY INSISTED.

Francis spread his hands. "He takes a toss off the horse, hits his head on a stone and can't do any better than crawl along a bit before he flakes out. So there he is lying unconscious in the bracken somewhere and, unless anybody searching is lucky enough to stumble over him, mighty difficult to see."

All this was poor comfort for Hooky and at half past six Rachel gave him his orders.

"Hooky, there is absolutely nothing more that you or any of us can do this evening. What you have got to do is to get into that marvellous old Jag of yours and take yourself off to the Huntsman in Exdale, and Hooky—"

"Half of what you feel like drinking will probably be enough."

It was very seldom that Hooky took orders from anybody about his drinking habits, but this time he nodded submissively.

"Entendu," he said, "and in case you don't know, that's a French phrase meaning you are a remarkable woman."

─────── ★ ───────

A Forthcoming Worldwide Mystery by
LAURENCE MEYNELL

HOOKY GETS THE WOODEN SPOON

DON'T STOP FOR
HOOKY HEFFERMAN

LAURENCE MEYNELL

TORONTO · NEW YORK · LONDON · PARIS
AMSTERDAM · STOCKHOLM · HAMBURG
ATHENS · MILAN · TOKYO · SYDNEY

DON'T STOP FOR HOOKY HEFFERMAN

A Worldwide Mystery/August 1990

This edition is reprinted by arrangement with
Scarborough House.

ISBN 0-373-26053-9

DON'T STOP FOR

HOOKY HEFFERMAN

ONE

'WELL, IF YOU ASK ME, I think the man must be mad.'

The remark was made in the small, over-heated living-room of a flat in Timmerton Square. Timmerton Square lies off Ebury Street. Even in today's hurly-burly of pressure and publicity the fifteen early Victorian houses of the Square manage to maintain an atmosphere of civilized seclusion.

Turn into the Square with its old-fashioned bow-windows, its elegant little balconies and the diminutive rectangle of 'pleasure garden' in the middle and you feel at once that London life can still, here and there, be conducted with some degree of dignity and even panache.

The interior of Charles Wilbury's ground-floor flat strengthened this conviction; but the modern pictures on the walls, the two rare pieces of French furniture, the exquisite little Waterford chandelier served as a reminder that Timmerton Square was not for the impoverished.

Not that Charles Wilbury was yet wealthy. He hoped to be one day, just as he hoped one day to be powerful, because he was ambitious; for the present he was making as much money as a brilliant young solicitor (he was thirty-two) could hope to make, and much more than the vast majority of his contemporaries in the law.

Everything he earned was deliberately being spent on what, in his own privately drawn-up formulation of policy, he called 'establishing himself'.

An essential part of this 'establishing' business was to secure a suitable London base; and 'suitable' in Charles Wilbury's vocabulary meant an impeccable address and surroundings, which would not only impress all his visitors but (to do him justice) would also give him the opportunity of living life as he thought it ought to be lived, in a civilized way among beautiful objects.

With the clear knowledge, therefore, that he was playing a long-term game for what he hoped would ultimately be big stakes, Charles had been bold right from the beginning.

He had not really been in a position to buy the outrageously expensive lease of the flat in Timmerton Square, but he had scraped together all that he could, mortgaged himself unmercifully and staked everything on the one throw.

Almost immediately, as though Fortune were shewing her approval of a bold player, luck came his way. The second partner in the old-established and prosperous firm of Oldmeadow, Williams & Wilbury died unexpectedly and Charles moved up from the most junior position long before he had any right to expect to do so.

Ever since getting into his flat he had spent all the money he could afford on buying beautiful things, and since he had innate good taste and was an extremely shrewd buyer he soon began to fill his small living-room with objects which delighted the eye.

Yet on this evening in early March, at the close of a London day in which there had been a welcome hint of spring, any impartial observer in that small room, looking round for a thing of beauty to rest his eyes on, would almost certainly have passed by the two Delagasse paintings, the marquetry and the cut glass, and concentrated on the girl of striking appearance who stood drink in hand, back to fire, head tilted backwards in characteristic pose, making her own assessment of things.

It was she who had said in her clear-cut incisive way, 'Well, if you ask me, I think the man must be mad.'

She had been christened, improbably enough, but these things happen, Annabella Fenella. At the highly expensive boarding school which she attended (and frequently scan-

dalized) attempts had been made to telescope this into An-
nella, but very early on in the proceedings she made very
clear what she wanted and was prepared to accept—*Fenella*.

It suited her, being slightly exotic and having a suggestion of something faintly foreign (Spanish perhaps?) which
went well with her dark colouring and the impression she
managed to give of smouldering vitality.

Had she lived in Michael Arlen's day she would undoubtedly have worn a small green hat.

Fenella D'Aubiac was a new phenomenon in Charles
Wilbury's life. So far he had had very little time for women.
He was a dedicated man, capable of an immense amount of
concentrated work. 'Dedicated' in Charles's case meant
being in the Lincoln's Inn Fields office by half past eight (the
staff didn't come in until nine); frequently lunching off a
sandwich and a cup of coffee brought in; and leaving at half
past six or seven with enough work in his briefcase to keep
him busy all evening.

Steady adherence to this programme, of which the late Mr
Samuel Smiles would no doubt have heartily approved, had
not left much room for girls; but this, again, had been a
piece of calculated planning on Charles's part. The scheme,
or *schema* as he preferred to think of it, had been: get your
honours degree at Oxford; as soon as you are through your
articles become a junior partner in a really high-class firm;
secure yourself an established base in London; begin to
make money in a meaningful way—then, and only then,
look round for a wife who would be of use to you in all you
want to do.

Most of this had gone—or, at any rate, was going—to
schedule; but the advent of Fenella on the horizon looked
like upsetting things considerably.

Fenella wasn't designed to fit into schedules. They had
met at one of those amorphous Chelsea parties at which the
stage, the screen, and the arts generally mix with the worlds

of politics, property and advertising; the style of dress being entirely idiosyncratic, the two strong cementing factors that bound the evening together being the worship of money and thirst.

Formal introductions were not used. 'You must know Fenella,' someone had said, which had brought Charles face to face with her for the first time.

'Who is that rather pompous man?' Fenella had enquired a quarter of an hour later.

'Charles Wilbury may be a bit pompous, my dear, but believe me he's going places. If he goes into politics, which he is said to be thinking of doing, he'll be what they call a coming man.'

Charles's second piece of luck (and there were moments of distraction when he almost thought of it as ill-luck) could be summed up in the one word *Loeson*.

He had just gone through a gruelling three-hour session in the cold, cavernous house up in Hampstead and it was his account of this frustrating, yet occasionally wildly funny, experience which made Fenella D'Aubiac say, 'Well, if you ask me, I think the man must be mad.'

Honesty, of which she possessed an embarrassing amount, had compelled Fenella to make considerable revision in her first estimate of Charles Wilbury.

A shade pompous—yes, she still thought him that; but she had to admit that he was also impressive. It was easy to understand the general view of him as 'a coming man'; but she was not at all sure that she wanted to share his journey.

She had taken the trouble to discover his age and had found him to be six years older than herself, which according to her reckoning (observation made her believe that the English Public School system generally retarded male development by about five years) put them on an almost equal footing.

At twenty-six she was that improbable phenomenon in this permissive day and age—a virgin. She had a long slender body, beautifully formed, and on horseback—she rode like Diana herself—she looked not less than superb. One day those lovely limbs of hers would delight some lucky man, but it would have to be a man who, in her own private phrase, 'gave off sparks'.

So far no sparks had come from Charles Wilbury; she found it hard to see him as the rip-roaring captain of a pirate ship which was still her way, remembered from childhood days, of estimating a hero.

Nevertheless there had been enough about Charles, plus the fact, difficult for any girl to ignore, that he was obviously interested, to make her agree to let him take her out to dinner.

The suggested programme was: pick Fenella up at her 'pad' in South Ken; half an hour or so for a leisurely pre-prandial drink in the Timmerton Square flat; then dinner, *à deux,* at Luigi's.

Charles suffered from the usual male delusion that he was a connoisseur of wine and good food; Luigi's at the moment was one of the 'in' places for these things and it had the added benefit that if you were spotted dining there you stood a good chance of getting a mention in one of the London gossip columns, particularly if your partner across the table was as striking looking as Fenella D'Aubiac; and although Charles was wont to deplore as loudly as anyone the vulgarity and cheapness of the daily press he never had the slightest objection to seeing his own name in it.

What Charles's ambitions might be after dinner Fenella didn't know. Not too masculinely aggressive, she hoped; men were apt to be tiresome in their cups.

Meanwhile there was his amusing, and in parts incredible, account of his Hampstead visit to listen to.

'In a way, yes, I agree Loeson probably *is* a bit mad,' Charles replied to her comment. 'It's arguable, I suppose, that all misers are a bit mad.'

'Is he really a miser? What fun!'

Charles laughed. It was easy to laugh when you were with Fenella; she looked at life in a cock-eyed way which found most of man's more serious activities amusing.

'Anyone who will sit in an overcoat and gloves rather than turn the central heating on because it costs so much looks pretty miserly to me, especially when you know that he must be worth somewhere between three and five million.'

Fenella had heard and read the word 'million' so often that she was not particularly impressed by it; and, in any case, her view of money was very different from that of Charles Wilbury. She admitted that it would be a nuisance to be entirely without the stuff, but she couldn't be bothered to make it number one on the agenda. All very foolish and impracticable, of course, which is probably why she enjoyed herself so much.

'I should think at least five million,' Charles amended his estimate in reverential tones, 'and possibly a good deal more. The old boy's so secretive that one doesn't really know.'

'If he's so tiresome, why work for him?'

'My dear girl, when a client worth that sort of money comes along you simply don't turn him down.'

Charles couldn't see Fenella open a small notebook and in its private pages make the entry of one large black mark for the simple reason that it was all done mentally. Fenella lived a good deal in the amused world of her thoughts. Her non-existent mental notebook had various titles: *Curious Customs and Beliefs of the Human Male; Particularly Objectionable Sayings; Puffed-up Platitudes from Peacock Land.*

She wasn't quite sure whether 'my dear girl' should be listed under the second or third of these headings; but it certainly belonged to one of them.

Naturally when Joseph Loeson had come, out of the blue, into the Lincoln's Inn office and asked for his affairs to be looked after by Mr Charles Wilbury in person he was not turned down.

Joseph Loeson, much as he might dislike publicity (and he disliked it very much indeed), was, after all, joint head of Vandeem Press Limited and Vandeem Press Limited was a big concern.

Just how big Charles learnt with growing astonishment and envy as his new client reluctantly disclosed an involved story of family quarrels, of deals and counter-deals and of furious disagreements with previous legal advisors.

Charles realized very early on that he was not being told everything and that he would not be in a position to do his best for his client until he was told everything. But meanwhile the fees were mounting up, extremely handsomely.

'The man's an extraordinary mixture,' he told Fenella. 'On the one hand there's this miser thing, the radiators not on and only one electric bulb burning in a huge drawing-room, and so forth; and on the other hand he has a visit from his doctor—and as a private patient at that—every single day.'

'Why, is he ill or something?'

'Not in the slightest. He's as tough as old boots. He doesn't smoke, he doesn't drink and he eats about half as much as the average human being, so of course he's almost indecently well. But he's a hypochondriac. He's quite convinced that there's something wrong with him; and if the doctor hasn't got the sense to find something wrong every few days, by God, he's given the sack and some other medico gets the job.'

'Has any poor misguided woman been fool enough to marry this sub-human?'

'He's a widower—'

'I'm not surprised. Did she commit suicide or was she starved to death?'

'And there's a boy aged fifteen or so.'

'Poor kid.'

'No; on the contrary. Loeson dotes on the boy. Anything the boy wants he's given; nothing's too good or too expensive. Well, after all, he can afford it.'

'Poor kid again; it's only fun being extravagant when you can't afford it. So what do you do exactly for this valuable and objectionable client of yours, Charles?'

Charles smiled. 'I hold his hand and charge him handsomely for doing so, which means that I have to be a combination of an R.C. priest, a psychiatrist and a top-class chartered accountant. Loeson's a mental hypochondriac as well as a physical one. He's convinced that everybody (but especially his cousin) is plotting to harm him in some way.'

'His cousin? Good grief, are there two of them?'

'Very much so. Ruben and Joseph Loeson. They own Vandeem Press between them; and believe me the articles of partnership are quite something; the document runs to sixty-four printed pages and if it ever got into court counsel would have a field day. Most of its articles can be construed in half a dozen different ways.'

'Why should it get into court?'

'What's worrying Loeson—*my* Loeson, Joseph—and why he came to me in the first case is the take-over. Have you ever heard of Market Enterprises Limited?'

'Vaguely. I think I have, yes.'

'Well, there's nothing vague about M.E. They are one of the really giant concerns—shipping, High Street stores, food, luxury flats, the lot. You name the pie, M.E. have got a hefty finger in it. And M.E. now want to get hold of Vandeem Press. Ruben wants the take-over, Joseph doesn't. That's the essence of the situation, and if that makes it sound simple believe me it *isn't*. Simple is the one thing this affair is *not*. Even if the two cousins were amiably disposed towards one another the business entanglements and complexities would be enormous, and when you get the sort of Cain and Abel atmosphere which exists between them everything is ten times worse. *My* Loeson, the Hampstead one, is genuinely afraid that cousin Ruben may employ some sort of strong-arm stuff. I think that's nonsense; but when a man's got persecution mania it's no good just telling him he's being silly.' Charles laughed and added, 'Besides, if I confined my advice to saying that, Mr Loeson might take his business elsewhere.'

'Let's hope nobody has taken over Luigi's,' Fenella said. 'I'm hungry.'

brrr-brrr, brrr-brrr

The shrillness of the sound was muted. Charles Wilbury recognized the telephone as an absolutely indispensable part of life, but he was civilized enough to want to keep the insistent intruder in its place. Consequently his instrument was not given space in his elegant little drawing-room but was housed in a cubby-hole off the hall.

With a word of apology to his guest he went out now to deal with it.

Fenella studied the two Delagasse pictures in turn—one on either side of the fireplace. She herself painted a little, and she could appreciate the technical skill of the canvases; but they were not to her taste. On the other hand they were probably valuable. No doubt lawyer Charles knew a lot about the value of modern pictures; just as he knew a lot about involved take-over bids and the like—how boring a great deal of the knowledge in the world is, she thought.

To judge by the time he was out of the room Charles seemed to be finding his telephone call troublesome, and when at long last he did return it was clear that he was upset.

Looking at his agitated face and listening (half-listening) to the beginnings of his embarrassed and stuttered explanation Fenella had a shrewd suspicion of what he was going to say.

'That was the old devil himself—Loeson.'

Fenella didn't propose to help him in his difficulties. She said nothing, merely watched and waited.

Charles was forced to abandon the cushioning of legal phraseology and to blurt out the awkward truth.

'I'm most frightfully sorry, Fenella, but he wants me up there. Now.'

'And are you going?'

'I *must*. He's in a dreadful state. It's that boy of his. Loeson's got himself convinced somehow that there's some sort of threat to the boy. He talks about danger—'

'Why doesn't he get in touch with the police?'

'My dear girl'—Fenella winced slightly—'the police! The last thing in the world Loeson would ever do would be to call in the police. He's got a phobia about them.'

'And what can you do?'

'God knows. But he wants me there. At once. He's hardly sane. Practically incoherent on the telephone.'

'Did you tell him you had a dinner engagement?'

'No, I didn't. No point in it. He's in such a state he would hardly have known what I was talking about. He wants me and I've got to go.'

'What about me?'

'Fenella—you can't think that I want to do this! But if I don't go and calm him down he'll almost certainly take his business away from the firm tomorrow.'

'And that would be dreadful, wouldn't it?'

'I'm certainly not going to let it happen if I can help it.'

'So it's good-bye to Luigi's?'

'Only for tonight, Fenella. I'm sure you understand....'

Fenella smiled sweetly, amiably and with an air of finality. 'I understand perfectly, Charles,' she said. 'Get my cloak and call me a cab, will you?'

TWO

IN HER CAB Fenella leant back, shut her eyes and smiled. She even gave one short laugh out loud. She was angry; and amused at herself for being angry; and mixed up with all this she even found time to feel sorry for Charles.

Poor, clever, civilized Charles, so dedicated to the sacred business of getting on.

'Shall I tell him to take you home?' he had asked, squiring her into the taxi with an over-zealous demonstration of solicitude and care.

'Of course not,' Fenella snapped. 'Tell him 15 Chessington Gardens.'

The 'pad' in a mews close to South Ken station was comfortable and she was happy in it; but having been done out of her expected taste of the *hig-lif* at Luigi's she had no intention of going back to the desolation of an empty flat and something hastily concocted over a gas-ring.

And being Fenella she had, as usual, a trump card in reserve.

No. 15 Chessington Gardens was a very nice trump to hold. Freddy and Holly Townsend lived there in cheerful domesticated disorder, with four children, two cats and a constantly changing assortment of other livestock and *au pairs*. The most obvious thing about the Townsends was that they were happy. Freddy put in an appearance at the House of Lords most days because the 'attendance money' of eight pounds a time formed a considerable part of his income; Holly, the plump, amiable, competent woman he had been sensible enough to marry, had already borne him four children, hoped to bear at least two more and quite unashamedly revelled in the never-ending womanly business of looking after them, him, the animals and the house.

On the face of things, 15 Chessington Gardens should have been the last place where huge, rambling, often semi-riotous parties were held which everyone in London who knew a good thing when they saw it wanted to attend. Yet the Chessington Garden routs had become famous; there was usually somebody amusing and unexpected there; and unfailingly there was always the refreshing atmosphere of a happy home content with simple things.

When Holly Townsend had rung her up and Fenella had had to say no, I'm going all smart for the evening, I'm being taken to dinner at Luigi's, Holly in her warm-hearted way had cried, 'But Freddy will be desolated. He dotes on you, Fen. He won't really regard it as a party without you.'

'Freddy's an angel, but to Luigi's I must go.'

'*Of course* you must. Lucky you. Or rather lucky somebody taking you.'

But now 'somebody' wasn't taking her to Luigi's and the taxi-cab driver, pulling up on the private road outside No. 15 said in the hoarse voice peculiar to his tribe, ''Ere you are, miss. Seem to be enjoying themselves in there.'

No. 15 Chessington Gardens was a tall, narrow, elegant-looking house which Freddy (who had no skill at making money and not much ambition in that direction either) could never have afforded. Luckily for him he didn't have to afford it; the house had been left in trust to him for his life by his grandmother, the famous old Marchioness, who disapproved of most things in the modern scene but who approved most heartily of Holly—'Just what Freddy needed,' the formidable old lady was wont to aver, 'a marmalade-making and mend-the-socks wife.'

Now out of the tall windows streamed light and such a concentrated hubbub of human sound that it was at once evident that the first basic essential of any successful party was being fulfilled—there were far too many people crammed into far too small a space for there to be any hope of comfort.

'What a row they're making,' Fenella said as she counted out the money for the fare.

The taxi-driver was an elderly Londoner; no modern equality nonsense for him; he reckoned to know class when he saw it; in his opinion young ladies who looked like Fenella ought to go to noisy parties and enjoy themselves.

'Don't worry, miss,' he assured her. 'They'll all go silent as soon as you walk in. Stunned like, they'll be. Knock 'em sideways you will.'

It was a charming compliment and Fenella, listening to it, couldn't be expected to guess how much inverted truth there would be in it.

She stood in the doorway of the long narrow drawing-room which ran the full depth of the house, and with a slight anticipatory smile on her face surveyed the noisy scene.

It continued to be noisy; so the taxicab-driver had been wrong, she thought.

'*Fen!* Holly told me you couldn't come.'

Her host's obvious pleasure was flattering.

'I was afraid I couldn't.'

'You were going to Luigi's, or somewhere—'

'I decided that this would be much more fun than Luigi's so I came here—is that all right, Freddy?'

'Darling Fen, *of course.*'

'What masses of people you and Holly seem to know, Freddy.'

'Awful, isn't it? The noise and the people. Rather fun though. I expect you know everybody.'

Fenella did indeed, if not actually know, at least recognize most of them. With the parties she went to it was apt to be a case of *plus ça change*; but then her eye, roving the animated scene, lighted on someone who was not by any means *la même chose*. Somebody that she didn't know. Looking at him she felt an undeniable little *frisson*; an alerted awareness; something half of the spirit, half of the body. How extraordinary, she thought, if the taxi-driver is going to prove right in reverse as it were.

'Mostly everybody,' she answered, hoping she was managing to keep her voice casually even, 'but who's that tall, chunky-looking man over by the window?'

The description amused Freddy. '*Chunky* is a very good adjective for Hooky Hefferman,' he said. 'That's just what he is.'

'A friend of yours, Freddy?'

'An acquaintance. In fact we were at Eton together. But we've gone different ways since.'

'What way has *he* gone—what did you say his name was?'

'Hefferman. Hooky. Hooky Hefferman.'

'And what way has he gone?'

Freddy laughed. 'I suppose you could say that I'm just a peace-loving domesticated family animal, and very happy with it all; but Hooky became a soldier of fortune. I see him looking over this way. Shall I introduce you?'

CHARLES WILBURY PAID off his cab and automatically made a mental note of the fare. In due course the 'nuisance factor', applicable in the case of rich and troublesome clients, would be invoked, that is to say the amount actually paid out would be multiplied by six and the resultant sum introduced under 'expenses' into the formidable half-year's bill for consultations and services rendered.

Stanmer Crescent was a quiet, discreet curve of expensive living in the hinterland of Hampstead. Large detached Victorian houses stood sombrely in their own grounds, withdrawn a little from the road, behind protective screens of laurels and fir trees.

After even more turning of keys and rattling of bolts than usual (Loeson was extremely burglar-conscious) the front door was opened sufficiently for Davis the houseman factotum to make sure who was there.

'Oh, it's you, Mr Wilbury. Thank goodness for that. He's been in a rare state waiting for you.'

'I came as soon as I could.'

'Of course you did, Mr Wilbury, but you know what he is.'

'What's it all about, Davis? What happened?'

'If you arsk me—nothing; but—'

'Is that you, Wilbury?'

The anxious cry from the drawing-room cut their conversation short, and instead of completing what he had been saying Davis rolled his eyes expressively and gave a jerk of his head. 'You'd better go in,' he said. 'He'll tell you.'

Entering the large, high-ceilinged drawing-room Charles was at once made aware of something unusual by the amount of light in the place. Generally Loeson was content to sit huddled over the fire with one single standard lamp doing inadequate duty for the whole big room, but this evening four lights carried in wall brackets were blazing as well.

The seated man looked up as Charles entered.

'I thought you would be here sooner,' he grumbled by way of greeting.

No apology, of course; no *Sorry if I disturbed your evening, good of you to come*; nothing like that; just the plain brutal assumption: *I've got money and I know you'll charge me heavily for doing what I want done so I expect you to do it.* Money ruled everything. . . .

In a curious way Charles Wilbury felt no resentment about this. It was an outlook that he understood. His own philosophy of life being directed entirely towards success was not so far different. Of course he was sorry to have had to forego this evening with Fenella, but girls, after all, who were all very well in their way, could always wait a little; business, especially business as important as Joseph Loeson, couldn't.

'I came as soon as I could, Mr Loeson. Actually I was just on the point of going out for the evening.'

'It's a good job I caught you in time, then. I want your help, Wilbury.'

'Anything I can do, Mr Loeson. Of course—'

'It's about Simon.'

When he pronounced the name of his fifteen-year-old son Loeson's voice took on a particular sort of urgency. There were two things which really mattered in life: making money and the welfare, or what he imagined to be the welfare, of his boy.

'Is he ill?' Charles enquired.

'Of course he's not ill,' Loeson snapped crossly. 'If the boy was ill, why you? I should send for a doctor, shouldn't I? Not that they do much for the money they charge these days, either. Simon's not ill; he's in danger.'

'In danger? What sort of danger?'

'I am quite certain the boy is in serious danger of being kidnapped.'

Charles stared at the unhealthy-looking figure hunched in the big armchair that so badly needed re-covering.... Kidnapped? A year or two ago the idea, the very word, would have seemed bizarre applied to London N.W.; now one couldn't be so sure. Anything was possible, one had to admit that; but even so....

'What makes you think that, Mr Loeson?'

'Simon has strict orders not to go out alone after dark, of course; if he goes anywhere, Davis should go with him. *Should, should, should,*' the word was repeated with almost frightening venom and bitterness. 'There's your world for you today. What should be isn't; what's laid down doesn't get done. You give orders and people are too busy, too much in a hurry, too couldn't-care-less to carry them out.

'So this evening Simon goes out by himself, in the dark, to the end of the Crescent where it joins Stanmer Hill Road and the shops are.

'To buy something. Always buying, buying, buying, that's boys for you today. Spending money.

'On his way back, halfway along the Crescent, where that big tree overhangs and it's dark a man spoke to him. Could Simon oblige him with a match? All very nicely spoken and friendly, apparently. Then at once into more talk. Who was Simon? and did he live nearby? In one of the big houses maybe? and had his father got a garden and was there any chance for a jobbing gardener?

'The boy began to come to his senses then and he got scared and ran away; home, here.

'He says he thinks the man ran after him, at least some of the way; but he suddenly became so frightened he isn't sure.'

'I suppose you haven't notified the police—'

'The police! Of course I have not notified the police. You know very well that's the last thing I would want to do. What use are the police to me? Big heavy men in uniform tramping about all over the house and grounds; and asking silly stupid questions. But all the same, mark you, *questions*. Am I wealthy? Such humour, with eighteen and sixpence in the pound I pay tax; who can be "wealthy" like that? What is my business? Who are my partners? What is the routine of the house? What? Why? When? Where? No; I want nothing of all that, thank you.'

'Perhaps the man was genuine.'

'Genuine? Yes, he was genuine enough. A genuine crook. I'm quite sure he was genuine.'

'He sounds to me more like a would-be burglar "casing the joint", as they call it, than anything else.'

'Possible; just possible. But it could be more than that. It could be worse. You play chess, Wilbury? This move counts. Right, of course it does. But anyone can make this move. The ordinary player knows enough to make this move. You don't get to be managing director and half-owner of all the shares and in the big business by being ordinary. By being able to see just this move. It's seeing the move ahead that counts. These last two years, these last few months even, how many kidnappings of rich men's sons have there been; tell me.'

'Quite a few,' Charles had to admit.

'So what do you imagine I have thought each time I read about one? I think: Joseph Loeson you are not different from anybody else; no one has given you a magic inoculation against disaster; I think *This could happen to you.*'

'But who would want—'

'Anyone who wanted to persuade me to sell my shares in Vandeem Press.'

'Your own cousin?'

'If you want to see a good strong feud with no holds barred look for a Jewish family that has split up. United? Yes, fine; everybody together and the old people looked after till they die. But if once there's trouble, if once they fall out—money, of course, will be the start of it—then, believe me, then they fall out in a big way, then there's trouble worth talking about. Do you know what I and my cousin Ruben quarrelled about?'

'No, I don't. I must confess I have sometimes—'

'You have sometimes wondered. All right, wonder. Why should I tell any family secrets to the outside world?'

'Mr Loeson, I feel justified in pointing out to you that I am not quite in the same position as what you call "the outside world". I am your solicitor whom you have engaged to conduct your private affairs.'

'All right, all right, all right. I agree, I agree. You are my solicitor, and a good solicitor too, else I don't employ you, do I? And pay you all the money you charge. And now I want your help. I ask you, will you please help me?'

'Yes, of course; I said earlier on, anything at all that I can do—'

'You think me silly. Maybe you are right. Maybe you are cleverer than me. Maybe I *am* silly. But silly or not I know what I feel; what I am afraid of. I think that there is a definite danger that someone—I name no names—someone may try to kidnap my boy whilst this fight about the shares is going on. I believe in signs, Wilbury, and in taking notice of warnings, and I feel it right here in my bones that what happened this evening in the Crescent was a warning. I am a fool if I don't take heed of it.'

'So what do you want me to do?'

'I want Simon to go away somewhere for a month, three months maybe. Myself I can't go. I must be here to fight for my control of the company, and to keep an eye on what you are all doing for the money I pay you. But Simon I want out of it.'

'Where?'

'Where? When? Why do you think I have asked you to help me? *I* don't know where. Hampstead I know and Eldon Place in the City. You think the boy should be hidden there maybe?'

'No, of course not.'

'Well, then, where? Somewhere in the Home Counties. You have a weekend cottage, or one of your extravagant friends has a weekend cottage. Small, tucked away, the village a mile off. Nobody knows who is there and who isn't. A fifteen-year-old boy comes as a guest, a friend of the family, who is he? Nobody knows or cares. Even his name isn't used. Never Loeson certainly; and not perhaps even Simon; by his second name he can be called, Leonard. And your friends who take the boy, what do they want to be paid? Don't answer me. I tell you it doesn't matter what they want to be paid. Thirty pounds a week, thirty-five pounds a week, forty even. All right, it doesn't matter. At such a price for what I am getting it is cheap. If you don't really want a thing it is dear at a penny; if it is something you want badly it is often cheap at a thousand pounds. My father taught me that. So tell me, where is this tucked-away cottage, this hidey-hole?'

'Not in the Home Counties,' Charles answered slowly; whilst his millionaire host was talking Charles had been thinking and a brilliant idea had just occurred to him. 'Anywhere in the Home Counties is too close to London and too crowded nowadays and too much everybody-knows-everybody-else's-business.'

'All right, I believe you. There are too many people in the world anyway. So you have somewhere else to suggest perhaps?'

'Yes, I think I have actually.'

'Tell me.'

'I've a—let me see—what is Francis exactly? He must be my first cousin once removed. Yes, that's it. I've a first cousin once removed. Major Francis Dobson. A good deal older than I am. Francis would be fifty or so now. They thought a lot of him in the Army, apparently, and he would have liked to stay on in it after the war but some bug had got into him out east and he was a pretty sick man so he had to take his bowler hat and his disability pension and get out. City life never suited Francis; neither his temperament or his health; and for the past ten years or so he has been living really right off the beaten track, in the middle of Exmoor, doing a bit of farming and watching birds and that's about all.'

'He lives alone, this cousin of yours?'

'Oh Lord, no. I don't think Francis could manage on his own. He's got a wife. A wonderful person, Rachel.'

'I like this name, Rachel. Why is she wonderful?'

'She looks after him so well. And she's a homely, domesticated creature. She's content.'

'You've been to this, what is it? cottage of theirs?'

'It's rather more than a cottage. In the old days it used to be a small farm. Yes, I've spent my last two holidays there.'

'And it is in the country?'

'Absolutely out in the wilds. You can be there and not see a single soul from the outside world all day long.'

'And they have a big family, your cousins?'

'No family at all. Much to Rachel's sorrow. She would love to have children; but there you are, it just hasn't happened. That's the way of things, isn't it? One woman couldn't care less about children and hates the idea of being bothered with them and yet can't stop conceiving; another one desperately wants a child, does all she can to get one and it never comes. Silly isn't it?'

'I am not responsible for the way the world is run. I've got quite enough to worry about with the affairs of Vandeem Press Limited. Don't blame me, Wilbury, for the way things are. And if I were you I wouldn't blame God either. After all, he's only human. Would this Major Dobson and his excellent wife with the good Jewish name have Simon to live with them for say two months, maybe three?'

'I feel sure they would. They occasionally take paying guests in the summer.'

'How much?'

The idea of Francis and Rachel Dobson had come into Charles's mind as an absolute inspiration, and the more he thought about them the more he realized what a perfect answer they were. Sheepsgate exactly fulfilled all the requirements laid down by the (as Charles was still inclined to think) over-anxious Loeson, and the addition of, say, fifteen pounds a week would be most welcome in a household where the budget was very slender. And, after all, why only fifteen after what had been said?

'How much?' Loeson repeated.

'I think I might be able to persuade them to take the boy for twenty.'

Loeson looked at him with a steady stare from eyes which were quite inscrutable; evidently the brain behind them was assessing, weighing, making judgment; it might be sardonic judgment, but the eyes gave away nothing.

'You think you could persuade then to do it for twenty pounds a week?'

'I think so. Yes.'

'And Major Dobson is a sick man?'

'*Was* a sick man when he left the Army. In fact that's why he left it, as I said. He was with Monty in the Eighth Army and Monty was very keen for him to stay on but Francis had this bug, or rather it had him, and the medicos said "No". But he's not a sick man now; he just has to take things easily, that's all.'

'He's not a robust man?'

'Robust? No, far from it. You certainly couldn't call Francis robust.'

'So now you have found a place for my boy to go, and I think it sounds a good place; but you must also find someone to look after him.'

'Someone to look after him?'

'Someone who *is* robust. Active, young. You don't imagine the boy is to be left to wander about all by himself do you?'

'A guard?'

'Call him tutor, then who suspects anything unusual?'

'He would have to be paid, of course—'

'Since when do I want a lesson from you in economics, Wilbury? Find me this man, that's all I ask.'

THREE

'HOOKY, I'M MAKING COFFEE. Are you coming up?'

Gloria Lefance's invitation, floating down from the top room of Regency House, came as a welcome interruption to the man on the floor below. Not that Miss Lefance brewed particularly good coffee, but going up the rickety stairs and drinking a cup with her at least provided an excuse for getting away from the sheets of foolscap on which the sentences formed themselves with such agonizing difficulty and slowness.

Agonizing and surprising.

It had all been such fun to do. Knocking about the world; taking the rough with the smooth, and generally speaking more rough than smooth; never refusing an encounter be it with freak, fanatic, or *femme fatale*; turning over the astonishing rag-bag of human life—all this Hooky Hefferman had found very easy in the doing; but it was proving mighty difficult in the telling.

Or, more correctly, in the writing.

The idea had been suggested to him in El Vino by one of the Fleet Street boys towards the end of a bibulous lunchtime session.

Hooky had had a sufficient number of Pimms Number One to make him talkative; and Hooky in the talkative stage was good value. A lot of it was true; and even when it wasn't strictly true it was *ben trovato*—you felt that if the girl hadn't actually come sliding naked down the banisters at that stage she should have done; the way Hooky told the story it would have been the appropriate gesture.

'I don't believe half of it,' the Fleet Street type had said, 'but it's damned funny. Why don't you get the old typewriter going and bash it out? *Confessions of a Private Eye*— actually I think that title has been used, and it isn't a particularly good one anyway. Still, no problem there; we can soon think up a title. I think I could guarantee four, probably six, articles in the *Sunday Screamer* and then you could shove a bit more on and make it into a book.'

The amiable mists of Pimms Number One made the idea seem attractive to Hooky and he said so.

'There's money in it, you know,' Fleet Street told him sagely. 'One way and another you have spent a lot of your life ferreting out dirt, and people like dirt. Just take a walk round the West End theatres and cinemas. You might make a packet.'

'I could do with it.'

'And, by the way,' Fleet Street warned, 'don't think I'm doing this for nothing. I gave up being a bloody philanthropist a long time ago. Literary agent in his spare time, that's me. Ten per cent and let somebody else sweat away at the writing.'

'Fix me up with a publisher and you can have your blood money,' Hooky told him.

So much effort was going into the business of getting it all down on paper that the term 'blood money' looked like being fully justified; and on this particular morning, as on so many mornings of Hooky's colourful life, things were not made any easier by the events of the previous evening.

It had been late enough in all conscience when he had left 15 Chessington Gardens. By that time he had become involved with a cheerful gang of night birds for whom clearly the evening was only just beginning. 'Why don't we all go on to Darling Duggie's?' one of them suggested.

'Why, is he giving a party?'

'Well, he will be when we turn up, won't he? We *are* a party. You'll come along, Hooky, won't you?'

The trouble with you Hooky is that enough is not enough. You never know when to say 'no'. The minatory sentence which he had heard his formidable aunt pronounce only too often flickered for a moment on the screen of Hooky's conscience; but the dragon was safely caged in her comfortable flat in Hove, and Hooky's conscience, never a very strong plant, was fighting a losing battle.

So Hooky had joined the revellers and they had descended *en masse* on Darling Duggie ('*déjà*-bloody-*vu*' Duggie, on account of his disenchanted outlook on life), and Duggie's ramshackle living-quarters had been ransacked of every single drop of liquid in them. 'You lot ought to hire yourselves out as one of the plagues of Egypt,' Duggie had told them. 'Locusts aren't in it with you'; and the clocks had been striking four in the thin, cold, morning air when Hooky had finally made his way back to Gerrard Mews in the heart of the jungle of Soho.

'I heard you come in last night,' Gloria Lefance said, 'or this morning, rather. Heavens, what hours you keep, Hooky!'

That amiable freebooter groaned slightly.

'I fell among thieves,' he offered in extenuation, 'and incidentally that might be a good title for my book.'

'What book, Hooky? Milk or black?'

'I've been fool enough to say I'll write my reminiscences—black, please—it's toil unimaginable.'

'You're not a writing animal, Hooky.'

'You can say that again.'

Hooky sipped the strong scalding-hot coffee and was grateful for it. Gloria Lefance had never had much success in life and clearly now never would have much success. How her theatrical agency survived at all was one of the many mysteries of Soho; yet somehow survive it did and, an uncomplaining, courageous fighter, she battled on.

She nursed a soft spot in her heart for Hooky; but that was the way of women with Hooky. They all had a soft spot in their hearts for him, and in his time he had enjoyed a lot of pleasant hours and garnered a great deal of trouble as a result.

'Where was the party last night?' Gloria asked.

'It started at the Townsends.'

'One of their famous "dos"?'

'One of their famous "dos",' Hooky confirmed.

'What fun. Who was there? Anybody special?'

Hooky took his time over lighting a cigarette and sending a smoke ring ceilingwards before he answered.

'There was a girl there—'

'Hooky, Hooky, with you there is always a girl there.'

Touché, Hooky thought, true enough; with me there is always a girl there; or nearly always anyway; but not always is there something special about her; and last night, at Freddy Townsend's, there surely had been something a little bit special about that one....

Freddy Townsend himself had brought her across the crowded room.

'Hooky, this is Fenella D'Aubiac.'

Young and dark and lovely; that was what Hooky thought immediately; clearly as English as they come, and yet with a hint of something in the ancestry behind her (a Spanish grandmother maybe?) more exotic. Steady, amused eyes, wise beyond their years, that were quietly summing him up.

'Do you often come to these parties?' she asked.

'Too often. I ought not to be here.'

'Nor I.'

'What should you be doing?'

'Dining at Luigi's with a man of law.'

'Your escort? Point him out to me.'

'He's not here. That's the point. In the end he couldn't make it. Big business reared its profitable head and I was deserted.'

'It's a grave mistake to let business interfere with life.'

'I shouldn't think you are often guilty of it.'

'Never. If work interferes with pleasure, give up work.'

'Wilde?'

'Quite possibly. Seeing he never did any, our Oscar was pretty good on the subject of work, like the famous one about work being the ruin of the drinking classes.'

'Which section are you in—drinking or working?'

'I work hard at drinking. At this very moment—didn't I tell you I ought not to be here?—I should be slaving away at my book.'

'You're an author?' The dark eyes, already dancing with amusement, widened a little in surprise.

'My God, no. Earn my living at it? Never; it's too much like hard labour. But one book I have been persuaded to have a go at. Egotistical, of course; but then you would expect that of me, wouldn't you? I *am* an egotist. And how can an autobiography not be egotistical anyway?'

'You are writing your autobiography?'

'I wish you didn't sound so amused at the idea. Yes, I am. Sort of. The Life and Hard-up Times of a Private Eye.'

'How exciting—are you really a private detective?'

'H. E. R. Hefferman, Regency House, Gerrard Mews, Gerrard Street, Soho, London, England. Private Investigator. Every sort of confidential enquiry or mission undertaken. In the present state of the market nothing too small. If you are going out for the evening and want a reliable, steady-going, reasonably sober person to mind your canary for you whilst you are enjoying yourself, let me know.'

'I haven't got a canary,' Fenella said, 'but I'll bear it in mind. Freddy told me you were a soldier of fortune and I liked the phrase. It suits you somehow; you look piratical....'

'True enough,' Hooky answered Miss Lefance, 'true enough. But all the same this one was a bit unusual. She told me I looked piratical.'

'She's got you summed up, then,' Miss Lefance said, much amused. 'You would make a damned good pirate, Hooky.'

Shortly after three o'clock that afternoon Hooky was again rescued from the toils of composition. This time by the caretaker, factotum and indispensable prop of the establishment, Roly Watkins, who, ascending the stairs from his grandiloquently named 'office' on the ground floor, poked his head into the room and enquired with relish, 'What 'ave you been up to then, Mr H.?'

Long experience had taught Hooky that it was no use expecting Roly to come straight to the point; like most semiliterate people he gloried in the approach devious.

But listening to Roly was better than struggling with sentences and paragraphs which refused to be assembled, so he leant back with relief and waited for enlightenment.

Roly consulted the small oblong card he was carrying.

'Oldmeadow, Williams & Wilbury,' he read out, as through uttering some magical incantation.

'What are you jibbering about, Roly?'

'Lincoln's Inn Fields. Solicitors. And one of 'em is down below waiting to see you. The one on this card, Mr Charles Wilbury. Seeing as 'e's Law I thought I'd better let you know first in case there's anything catching up with you like.'

Colourful though much of his contact with life had been, Hooky couldn't think of any episode from the past which threatened to 'catch up with him' at the moment and in his present state any diversion was welcome. He stretched out his hand for the card that Roly was carrying and consulted it for himself; he was curious to know what Charles Wilbury of Oldmeadow, Williams & Wilbury, Solicitors & Commissioners for Oaths, might want.

'Tell this lawyer bird to come up,' he said.

The lawyer bird at that moment was feeling slightly dubious. Regency House was picturesque rather than impressive, and Charles Wilbury was beginning to wonder if he were on the right track.

On the previous evening it had been ten o'clock and later when he had finally managed to get away from Hampstead. What his rich client wanted could be stated simply enough, but with the arrogant dominance of wealth Loeson had kept on reiterating it, and having been said twenty times already it formed the substance of his final sentence of the evening, 'Now, don't forget Wilbury; I want all this fixed up at once. At once. Simon I tell tomorrow morning to start packing. These cousins of yours, get on to them tonight. Never mind about the money. Money is nothing—my God, listen to me! the things one is reduced to saying, but that's how it is. And the tutor-guardian-companion let me know who he is by tomorrow night. Here. You come up to tell me everything is fixed, eh? Somebody active—strong. Somebody to be a friend with the boy. What do I have to pay such a tutor? Don't tell me. Like I said, it doesn't matter. Just get it all arranged. Tomorrow. Three weeks' delay and difficulties and we'll-see-what-can-be-done—none of this I want; all this stuff is for firms I don't employ; the firm I pay so much money to to do my business as I pay you, I want that business *done*, at once.'

Charles didn't, in fact, telephone Sheepsgate until just after eight o'clock next morning. He had no difficulty in getting through and his cousin's agreeable cultured voice might have been in the next room, so clear it was.

'Francis? Charles Wilbury here. Is Rachel about?'

'She's on the moor, exercising her horse.'

'You energetic people. How are you off for P.G.s, Francis?'

'Haven't got any unfortunately. Things have gone very slack.'

'Good, good. That's excellent. Now listen, Francis. I've got a couple of P.G.s for you and I want you to have them for three or four weeks anyway. Might be quite a bit longer. Can Rachel manage that?'

'I'm sure she can. What are they, a married couple?'

'No. A boy of fifteen and a man to be a sort of companion to him.'

'Is the boy all right? I mean he isn't a mental defective of some kind is he?'

'Good Lord, no. Nothing like that. Very much the reverse I should say. His father wants him out of London for a few weeks. Country air. And the man with him is a kind of tutor really; keep the boy interested and perhaps do a bit of reading together and so on. I know the boy's father quite well; he's a client of mine.'

'I'm sure Rachel will be pleased about it, Charles.'

'What are you charging these days?'

'As you know I leave all the office side of things to Rachel. I call her the Home Secretary. I just get the firewood in and wash the dishes. She'll talk with you about terms; of course, as it's for a friend of yours we'll make it as low as we can, but I think we came to the conclusion that with the price of food the way it is the least we can possibly ask now is nine pounds a week.'

'Eighteen a week for two?'

'As there are two and it's going to be for some little time I suppose we might manage to make it, say, seventeen a week.'

'Don't bother to start cutting it down, Francis. My client is willing to pay thirty pounds a week.'

'Thirty pounds a week! I can't tell you, Charles, what a godsend that's going to be. We've been living in a very meagre fashion lately.'

'That's fine, then. Regard it all as fixed. I'll ring you up again this evening to tell you when they are coming. I expect it will be tomorrow.'

'Tomorrow?'

'Almost certain to be, I should think. And before I ring off—I suppose Sheepsgate is just as remote as ever? Nobody's built a housing estate near you or anything like that?'

'Housing estate? Good heavens, no. We seem to be more in the wilds than ever. An occasional hiker goes past once in a while, but often enough a whole week goes by and we don't see a soul.'

'Excellent, excellent. I'll be on the line again this evening.'

The news from Exmoor had pleased Charles enormously. It might have happened only too easily that Sheepsgate was already booked up with P.G.s and could do nothing to help him, but the Fates were on his side; it was a good omen.

He set off for Lincoln's Inn Fields well pleased with the day so far. He had made a good start. It wasn't everybody, he preened himself, who at the drop of a hat could produce an ideal hidey-hole like Sheepsgate. Of course, the problem of getting a suitable companion for the boy remained and he could see that to do that as quickly as his employer was insisting that it must be done wasn't going to be easy.

At nine o'clock he rang the flower shop in the Burlington Arcade; although the evening at Luigi's had had to be sacrificed in the sacred cause of business he had no intention of abandoning Fenella altogether and he made his placatory offer of lunch so contritely that she laughingly accepted his apologies and agreed to be at L'Ecu at one o'clock.

The morning proved troublesome and frustrating, and towards the end of it Charles was beginning to sweat a little. Suitable tutor-companions who would be willing to bury themselves in the wilds of Exmoor for an unspecified time evidently didn't grow on trees. Loeson had already been on the telephone once and had given four o'clock in the afternoon as the deadline by which he expected to hear that the whole thing was satisfactorily settled.

'I'll certainly do my best, Mr Loeson; but I am sure you will appreciate that you are giving me very little time.'

'Time, time! Always people finding excuses. What do I read about half a million people unemployed?'

'But Mr Loeson, they aren't *suitable* people. You don't want just anyone for this post. You want somebody young-ish, educated, intelligent, with a good background, trust-worthy.'

'So I think of you, Wilbury, don't I?'

'Of *me*?'

'Naturally. You are all these things you speak of other-wise I don't pay you to be my lawyer.'

'But Mr Loeson—'

'Why can't you take all these books and papers and doc-uments you have to read down to this lovely old farmhouse where your cousin is and work there in peace and quiet?'

'I—it—I—'

'Like this I am perfectly satisfied.'

'Mr Loeson, I'll ring you again at four and I hope I shall be able to tell you then that something satisfactory has been arranged.'

All very well to talk like that, firmly and decisively and as nearly dismissively as he allowed himself to be when deal-ing with a rich client, but by the end of the morning noth-ing satisfactory had been arranged. In fact nothing whatever had been arranged.

Charles arrived at the luncheon rendezvous in Jermyn Street looking, as Fenella was amused to observe, unchar-acteristically harassed.

It was a spring day and Fenella herself looked the very essence of spring, slender and lissom with that bewitching smile of hers; if you remembered your Meredith you thought of his 'dainty rogue in porcelain'.

'The man of law looks worried,' she teased him. 'You shouldn't have gone off to see that miserable old client of yours yesterday evening, Charles.'

'How right you are! My God, what these people expect for their money.'

'No doubt it's good money.'

'I'll see to that; believe me, I'll see to that when the account goes in.'

'What did the ogre of Hampstead want?'

'Just a moment,' Charles said. 'Let us deal with what we are going to eat first.' Charles Wilbury had very sound ideas on the question of food and drink; the fact that half the world was starving was no good reason, in his opinion, why the other half shouldn't do themselves as well as they could. He considered the menu critically and carefully.

'There's paté de fois gras . . .' he suggested.

The small shapely head shook decisively. 'No. Never. One of my principles. Beastly. the way they get it, I mean. It ought not to be on the menu.'

'Ah, principles; that's different, of course. Well, in that case let us opt for elegant simplicity. Asparagus—'

'Lovely. I adore asparagus.'

'And fresh Scotch salmon.'

'Marvellous.'

'Or, I tell you what,' Charles amended, turning excellence into perfection, 'why don't we start with an avocado, then the salmon and have the asparagus as a separate dish to end up with?'

'I forgive you for not taking me to Luigi's last night.'

'And will you leave the choice of wine to me?'

'Of course. I find the sight of a man poring earnestly over the wine list extremely amusing. Personally I don't mind what I drink.'

A shade passed over Charles Wilbury's urbane features; he perceived, dimly, that even a goddess can have a flaw.

When the avocado was disposed of Fenella repeated her question, 'And what did the ogre of Hampstead want?'

'It's that boy of his—you know what the chosen race is about its children. Simon is the apple of his father's eye. At the same time the old man is convinced the boy is a spendthrift good-for-nothing devoid of every single virtue of his tribe. He is equally convinced that the boy is in danger—'

'*Is* he in danger?'

'Personally I doubt it. But, to be fair to Loeson, I suppose one has to admit that it's possible. The world being in the state it is these days one simply doesn't know.'

'And what are you expected to do about it?' Fenella enquired.

'I've already done it,' Charles replied with that touch of smug self-satisfaction which only too often invaded his manner. 'What Loeson asked me to find was a comfortable home, tucked well away in the country miles away from the London scene, run by nice people where the boy can be lodged as a P.G. for a month or perhaps even longer. I was able to tell him, straight away, right off the cuff, that I knew of just the place.'

'Clever you.'

'Not bad, was it? A bit of luck, you might call it, I suppose; but there you are. I *am* lucky. If I take finesses at bridge they nearly always come off.'

'Bridge seems to me to be one of the final idiocies of the human mind. Where is this wonderful place you had up your sleeve?'

'Away down in the West Country. A cousin of mine. Ex-Army type. A first-rate chap, but pretty groggy physically. He does a bit of token farming and his wife takes in P.G.s to help out. I've been on the phone to them already and it's all signed, sealed and delivered.'

'So there's joy in the Hampstead synagogue?'

'Except, of course, for the tutor-companion, or whatever you like to call him.'

Fenella raised interrogative eyebrows.

'Is that why you arrived looking worried?' she asked.

'Yes, it is. Mind you I think Loeson's right. Given the validity of his premise that the boy is in some sort of danger, he *is* right. What he wants me to find now—what he has told me I have *got* to find, and I can't say I relish being spoken to like that, but there are some clients one can't risk offending although I must admit—'

'Who was it, Charles, who said that verbosity is the mother of boredom?'

'I haven't the faintest idea, and I'm sorry if—'

'Don't get huffy, Charles. You're giving me such a splendid lunch and I am enjoying it all so much. You know just exactly how to order a meal. There, that makes you feel better, doesn't it? You can't be huffy after that. Now tell me about this tutor-companion business.'

'Well, there will have to be someone to look after the boy; keep an eye on him; act as a companion; perhaps do a bit of tutoring. Francis Dobson—that's my cousin down there—can't do it. For one thing he's got his farm to look after and for another he isn't fit. I do see that we want a companion for the boy and I don't need Loeson to tell me the sort of person we want; but what he won't understand is that even I can't guarantee to lay my hands on exactly the right man at a few hours' notice.'

'And if you can't do it, Charles, who can?'

'Exactly. Give me a week or ten days and I'll find somebody but Loeson wants the answer today, by four o'clock. I've come up with the ideal place; but this other thing....' Charles shook his head and took a consoling sip from his glass.

'The sort of person you want', Fenella said reflectively, 'is someone with a good background, say an O.E.; youngish; pretty tough and used to a certain amount of dirty work, a sort of private eye in fact.'

'My dear girl, I don't have to be told what I want. I know what I want. Of course, the sort of man you are describing would be perfect, but where do I find him?'

'And if he were in the middle of writing a book and would welcome, say, a month's banishment to the back of beyond that would be ideal.'

'My dear girl, ideals like that just don't happen.'

'That's twice, Charles.'

'Twice what?'

'Twice in as many minutes that you have used that fatuous phrase "my dear girl". I find it intensely irritating. Never mind; don't let's spoil a lovely lunch. And cheer up because this particular ideal *has* happened. You may be good at finding the right sort of place for the boy to go to; I've got his tutor-companion for you.'

'You have?'

'Mr H. Hefferman. Regency House. Gerrard Mews, Soho. Every sort of enquiry or confidential mission undertaken—as far as I can remember, I think that's how he put it; and I must say he looks the part. Why don't you call and see him?'

Charles was already glancing at his watch.

'May I use your name and say you recommended him?' he asked.

Fenella laughed her clear, bright laugh. 'Yes, you can say I recommended him,' she agreed. 'He's the sort of man I would recommend for quite a number of things.'

His first impression of Regency House slightly dampened Charles Wilbury's ardour, but once Roly Jenkins had escorted him upstairs and he found himself confronted by the powerfully built individual on the other side of the desk in the small room on the first floor he felt reassured.

'Mr Hefferman?' he asked.

'*Me voici.* But Hooky to the initiated.' (Hooky pointed to his twice-broken nose, an ungainly yet curiously attractive feature of a rugged face.) 'And you are'—he consulted the card once again—'Charles Wilbury?'

'Of Oldmeadow, Williams & Wilbury, Lincoln's Inn Fields.'

'Excellent. Lawyers are always welcome. People don't go to lawyers unless they are in trouble of some sort and other people's troubles are my business.'

'I understand that you are what I believe is known as a private investigator....'

Hooky nodded.

'Well, I don't want any investigation done, Mr Hefferman, but there is a—I suppose you would call it a *job*—a responsible job—which you might be prepared to carry out for me.'

Hooky lit a cigarette and blew a perfect smoke ring up towards the ceiling. 'Let's hear about it,' he said encouragingly. 'Spill the beans.'

'I have a client....' In carefully rounded sentences, embellished with well-chosen words, Charles Wilbury detailed the position. Hooky listened in growing astonishment that any disbeliever could still maintain the age of miracles to be over. What was being described sounded to him like the perfect assignment, the answer to an impecunious private eye's dream, and he had virtually decided to accept even before the lawyer finished speaking.

But a certain amount of ferreting and fencing remained to be done.

'But *why*?' he asked. 'I don't quite get the "why" of all this. Is the boy going to the country merely for his health?'

'No, he isn't, Mr Hefferman. I'll be frank with you. His father is a rich man. A very rich man. And at the moment he is engaged in some very delicate business negotiations. He is also a Jew. One way and another he has got this phobia about kidnapping fixed in his mind. Either by business rivals or by one of these Arab guerilla movements.'

'Do you think the boy is in danger of being kidnapped?'

'No, I don't. But you can't be sure. It's a possibility. And anyway his father wants him safely out of the way and is prepared to pay for it.'

'That's always good news. What age did you say the boy is?'

'Just fifteen.'

'And I shall have to be on hand most of the time?'

'Keep an eye on him, yes. See that he doesn't go wandering off by himself. Notice if there are any suspicious strangers about. That sort of thing. But of course you'll have to have reasonable time off as it were and, after all, my cousin and his wife will be there as well.'

'What about the tutoring? "B.A. failed" is about the extent of my scholastic achievement.'

'I don't think we need bother too much about that side of it. Perhaps a bit of reading together to pass the time. Just being there is the main thing.'

'A moment or two back you spoke about your client being prepared to pay—how much?'

'Well now, that's probably going to be a matter of negotiation, isn't it? I'm sure you will appreciate that certain advantages go with this particular job; you will be living in a comfortable house with a civilized host and hostess and no expenses of any sort. And I feel certain you will have ample opportunity for writing your book.'

'What book?'

'I understand you are writing your reminiscences.'

'How the hell do you know that?'

'Miss Fenella D'Aubiac told me. It was she who recommended your name to me.'

'Was it indeed?' Hooky looked more closely at his visitor. 'Are you the man of law who ought to have taken Fenella to Luigi's last night but stood her up?'

'If you care to put it that way.'

'Well, well, well. It's a small world, isn't it? Right-o, then, about the money: as you say, I shall be living comfortably and without expense, and on top of that I want my fee, ten quid a day.'

Wilbury considered for a moment in silence. To part with ten pounds a day for any purpose would not be pleasant for Joseph Loeson, but on the other hand it would not in fact make any appreciable difference to his income; and with luck and the help of a skilful accountant it might be possible to set it off as an expense against income-tax liability.

He nodded. 'I expect that will be all right.'

'And when do I start?'

'Almost certainly tomorrow. I'll get on to the boy's father right away and ring you some time this evening.' The lawyer rose to leave, but he had one more thing to say.

'Just one last thing,' he said. 'Secrecy. If anyone wants to know where Loeson's boy is, ''With friends, somewhere in the country'' is the answer. Nobody should be told the exact address.'

'Don't worry,' Hooky reassured him. 'You've hired yourself a private eye, not a blabbermouth.'

FOUR

THE WAY TO SHEEPSGATE was, as the local wiseacre in the square of Exdale explained, 'frightfully simple'; it was also, as Hooky discovered, suffering in sympathy with his ancient and beloved motor-car, simply frightful.

'All you do,' the wiseacre explained, 'is turn right over the bridge here; follow the road over the moor till you see the sign; branch left, and there you are.'

Thankful for such straightforward instructions Hooky let in his clutch and started to move out of the tiny moorland town.

'Turn right over the bridge the man said,' the fifteen-year-old boy reminded him in the bright, know-all tone of voice which Hooky had already begun to find tiresome.

'I know, I heard him,' he growled.

'Road over the moor' the man had called it; the thing they were travelling along might well go over the moor, Hooky thought, but it was a gross exaggeration to refer to it as a road.

'Sort of place where you are quite likely to break a spring, I should think,' Simon said happily. 'Depends on the degree of tension you've got them at, of course. On some of the good modern cars you can vary the spring tension. Can you do it on yours?'

Hooky restrained himself; his job, he reflected, was to look after this exasperating youth, not to belt him one under the ear.

'I expect we'll manage,' he said.

When Exdale was some four miles behind them and they had not seen a human being, a building or even as much as a tree for some time a solitary object shewed up at the roadside.

An ancient signpost, leaning at a crazy angle after being battered for generations by the south-west gales, pointed to a track leading off to the left. The lettering, which was well over a hundred years old, was still decipherable. 'Sheepsgate Only,' it said.

Reluctantly Hooky swung his bonnet to the left; the moorland road they had been travelling on was a smooth and shiny highway compared to the track they had now to follow. It was entirely unmetalled and deep formidable ruts followed one another in alarming frequency.

Hooky engaged bottom gear and, with a silent prayer of apology to the good craftsmen and true who had put his Jag together, soldiered on.

'I think we probably *shall* break a spring here, shan't we?' Simon chanted. 'What fun!'

Several terse replies formed themselves in Hooky's mind, but he suppressed them; he could see that his ten pounds a day was going to be hard-earned money.

After three-quarters of a mile of what was to any car-conscious mind torment the track they were on rose sharply to a crest and, that crest once gained, they found themselves looking down at the house.

Sheepsgate.

Built of stone to last; built low to avoid the winds which in winter time blew harshly here; snuggling up against the side of the moor which rose steeply behind it, the place had something simple, elemental, satisfying about it.

Hooky liked the look of it from the word 'go' and was prepared to forget the nightmare of the last twenty minutes.

There was a fence of sorts and a white gate.

'Well, here we are,' Hooky said. '*Arrivati* as the Eyeties say. We've made it. What are you waiting for?'

'Waiting?' the boy asked.

'Hop out and open the gate,' Hooky told him. 'It won't open by itself.'

SUCH WAS HOOKY'S ARRIVAL at Sheepsgate. After he had been there a week he had to admit that in many ways the place fascinated him.

Cockney sparrow that he was, city bred and inured to the deafening lunacies of traffic, he had forgotten that such peace and solitude existed.

The small, solid farmhouse sat—squatted would be a better word—in the very lap of the moor. The one dubious track leading to it was the only thing that broke the sea of short, sweet, springy turf stretching away on every side, from the very edge of the farmyard for as far as the eye could see.

A man might sit in the sunshine outside the open front door all day long (as Hooky discovered) and beyond the small domestic noises of the house itself hear not a sound except the gentle sighing of the wind across the turf, and thin and far away the sheep bleating on the hillside.

The visit of the postman (some time between ten o'clock and midday, and not every day at that) was almost their only contact with the outside world, and when evening came and the huge log-fire was blown into a blaze by a pair of antique bellows silence reigned supreme.

'I'm afraid you'll find it frightfully dull,' Rachel Dobson said, 'but we love it here.'

Hooky liked his hostess from the first moment of meeting her. Rachel was plain and homely. She was perpetually busy and perceptually cheerful; and she smelt of good things, of elemental things like baking bread, or tending a sickly lamb in the kitchen, or bedding down the horse.

Moved to admiration by her unending labours and unvarying cheerfulness Hooky said to his host, 'By God, you've got a treasure of a woman there, Francis.'

Francis, gentle appreciative Francis, nodded. 'Don't I know it,' he agreed. 'Why don't you get yourself a wife, Hooky, and learn how good life can be?'

After a moment's reflection Hooky answered in an unusually self-analytical mood. 'Because I'm a tearaway sort of devil,' he said. 'Women—oh Lord, yes, I've had lots of fun with lots of women, and they with me, I think I can claim that; but I don't think I'd be much cop as a permanent partner.'

Francis Dobson laughed and pushed the whisky decanter across the table. 'Well, Rachel thinks a lot of you,' he said, 'and, if I may say so, so do I. It's nice having you here, Hooky.'

It was nice being there. If he had had to look forward to spending the rest of his days at Sheepsgate Hooky might well have taken a different view of the matter but for the five or six weeks that he expected to be there he knew the place would suit him very well.

Being a professional and a great believer in giving value for money his first concern had been to study the place from a security angle.

Already it seemed probable that the fifteen-year-old Simon (the 'Leonard' business suggested by the boy's father had never been adopted) was going to turn out to be a particularly vexatious cross to bear; but Hooky had undertaken to keep an eye on his charge and he intended to do it.

The more he took stock of the situation the more it looked like a piece of cake.

His first problem had been how much to tell the Dobsons. From the start he liked them both so much and they were so patently people of honesty and integrity that he was very much tempted to tell them the exact truth of the matter. On reflection, however, and on the general principle that it is never wise to put all one's cards on the table, he decided that some explanation rather less dramatic-sounding than a tale of possible kidnapping would be best.

'I expect you are wondering exactly why Simon's father has packed him off down here,' he suggested on the first evening when, the boy being in bed, the three of them were sitting by the soft light of the oil lamp (Francis disliked electricity) in front of the crackling fire.

'I suppose just a holiday?' Rachel suggested tentatively.

'In a way, yes. But there's a bit more to it than that. You know how close-knit Jewish families often are and how, if they do have a row, it tends to go deep and be lasting; well, there's some sort of trouble between the boy's father and an uncle and until it's all settled up the father wants Simon out of the way so he won't get involved in it.'

'Jolly sensible idea.'

'Yes. The point about it is, though, the father doesn't want anyone to know where the boy is. You don't have a daily help, do you?'

Rachel laughed. 'We don't have anybody. Just ourselves and of course an occasional P.G. in the summer. We could have a herd of performing elephants here and I don't suppose a single soul in Exdale would be any the wiser.'

'Is there anybody nearer than Exdale?'

'Only Castlecroft. That's a house on the far side of the Lonely Barrows; over the moor; about three miles away. An out-of-the-way place even by moor standards. It stood empty for a long time; then a couple came there three or four months ago—'

'Do you know them?'

'It sounds frightfully unneighbourly but, do you know, I've never even set eyes on them. I just heard they were there from gossip at the W.I.'

'They don't come over this way at all?'

'They don't seem to go anywhere. I have heard that she rides a bit, but I've never seen her. You certainly won't be troubled by them.'

'And this W.I. gossip—you won't be telling them all about Simon taking refuge from his family quarrels here?'

'I shan't say a thing, Hooky; and, in any case, the next meeting isn't for another month.'

'Excellent.'

'And, Hooky,' Rachel interrupted her task of darning one of her husband's socks long enough to make her next point, 'may I suggest something?'

Hooky grinned. 'Always open to suggestions from attractive women,' he said. 'What's yours?'

'Just relax. That's all. You have absolutely nothing to worry about. Neither Francis or I will say a word to anyone about Simon being here; so if the boy's father says nothing nobody will know. And as for casual visitors they just don't happen. Most boys like knocking about on a farm and I'm sure Simon will be happy going round with Francis and doing bits of odd jobs with the animals. I discovered a long time ago, Hooky, that most of the things one worries about in life don't really exist.'

Taking good advice wasn't one of Hooky's strong points, but he found quiet, competent Rachel a convincing sort of person and he thought that what she said made good sense.

Indeed, what she had prophesied that first evening immediately began to come true, at least in part. The cowshed, the pigsty and the stables were an entirely new world for the fifteen-year-old boy, and for a good part of each day he seemed happy enough going round with Francis and giving a hand when asked to do so.

The fly in the ointment was that between Hooky himself and the boy there was absolutely no *rapport*. Hooky had the sort of tolerant philosophy which made it easy for him to get on well with most people he came across, but at Sheepsgate he found his tolerant philosophy deserting him. Simon Loeson, the ludicrously spoilt son of an exceedingly rich father, the fifteen-year-old sarcastic know-all, was proving a severe trial. Attempting genial conversation with him was like trying to get on intimate terms with a particularly unresponsive hedgehog.

There was the occasion, for instance, of the great sheep round-up. Francis wanted to take advantage of having two extra helpers available to gather his dispersed animals from off the hillside and corral them in the small hurdled enclosure by the house where he could examine them for foot-rot.

The sheep were unco-operative and the operation involved a great deal of shouting and repetitive running to and fro on the hill, all of which Hooky found exhausting but enjoyable.

'Run,' he screamed at Simon, who should have been able to cut off the escape of a particularly obstinate old ewe.

Simon didn't run, and the ewe triumphantly escaped, to let them all in for a further ten minutes' work. Ultimately she was rounded up with the rest, and Hooky, panting, said, 'If you had run when I shouted you could have stopped that black-faced old devil getting away.'

'The whole affair seems to me to be so badly organized,' the boy said. 'It isn't scientifically arranged at all.'

'Good grief, boy, this is the middle of Exmoor, not a school laboratory. Who the hell wants scientific arrangement here? All this charging about is pretty desperate work, I'll grant you, but it's good for us.'

'It may be good for you,' Simon said, 'because you drink so much whisky, but I should think you are very liable to have a heart failure if you do much of it.'

'My heart has stood harder shocks than this, sonny, don't you worry.'

'Oh, I'm not worried. I'm just interested in observing things, that's all. And sheep are such silly creatures, anyway.'

Hooky laughed. 'Maybe. Somehow I got quite fond of them when I was in Australia.'

'What were you doing in Australia?'

'Knocking about.'

'I don't think I should like the Australians.'

'Maybe the Aussies wouldn't be altogether mad about you.'

'Did you make any money out there?'

'Not so you would notice it.'

'There wasn't much point in going there, was there? I intend to make a lot of money when I grow up.'

Hooky nodded. 'I should think you will very likely succeed,' he said.

It was the stable that proved the greatest attraction to Simon. The boy had never in his life been on a horse, but for some reason or other the sight of Rachel saddling up and putting the bridle on her mare fascinated him.

Cinders, a fifteen-hands bay with an uncertain temper and an awkward action, was Rachel's one personal extravagance. In spite of the constant pressure of domestic duties she managed to escape nearly every day for an hour's riding over the moor, and Simon was very soon nagging her to let him go out on the mare.

'I do wish you would explain to the boy that I simply can't let him take Cinders out,' Rachel said to Hooky. 'If I had another horse and we could go out together it would be different; but I daren't let an absolute beginner go out on that tricky mare of mine. It just wouldn't be safe. The trouble is Simon won't take "no" for an answer.'

Simon listening, looked bored, whilst Hooky somewhat forcibly repeated the substance of all this to him.

'I really don't see why not,' he said when Hooky had finished.

'Well, for one thing you don't know one end of a horse from the other.'

'I suppose you learnt all about horses in Australia?'

'I learnt quite a bit about doing what the boss said.'

'What boss?'

'Down here, chum-o, and as far as you are concerned, *I'm* the boss. *In loco parentis,* that's me; and in case you've forgotten your Latin that means be a good boy and do as you're told and we can all get along happily together. So, if Mrs Dobson says *no riding*, there it is, that's it, no riding, O.K.?'

However, these verbal brushes with his charge did not take place all the time, and by and large Hooky felt that things were going well.

At the end of his first week at Sheepsgate there were two remarkable circumstances upon which to reflect. The first was that seven whole days had gone by in which he, literally, had not spent a single penny; and the second that he was seventy pounds better off.

A third agreeable circumstance arose that evening shortly after six o'clock. Earlier in the day Simon had discovered a chessboard and set.

'I suppose you don't play chess, do you?' was his approach to Hooky.

'I'm afraid I'm not brainy enough.'

'Quite so,' the boy nodded. 'Oh, well, it can't be helped.'

But it turned out that Francis was fond of the game and was only too glad to have found an opponent. At six o'clock he said to Hooky, 'Why don't you take the evening off, Hooky? Simon and I are going to have a game of chess, so we shall be indoors with Rachel and there's no earthly reason why you shouldn't take yourself off for a few hours.'

It sounded a very sensible suggestion to Hooky.

'Is there a pub round about?' he asked.

Francis laughed. 'Hardly "round about",' he said. 'The nearest is in Exdale. The Huntsman. It's tucked away a bit—'

'Don't worry,' Hooky assured him. 'I'll find it.'

EXDALE WAS A DARK and secretive little place at the best of times; when night came down on the moor the town shut its doors, pulled its curtains, withdrew into itself, and wanted to have very little to do with strangers who shouldn't be abroad at that sort of hour anyway. Its streets were narrow and full of unexpected twists and corners and the Jolly Huntsman was hidden away in one of the least accessible of these crannies.

Hooky, however, had no difficulty in finding it. Instinct guided him to it unerringly. For Hooky was your true pub-lover; he understood the basic philosophy of the pub; for him a pub was the friendly corner into which a man grate-fully sank for restorative treatment after a gruelling three minutes with Life in the roped square.

Turnabout Street was dark and in itself unpromising, but halfway down it the splendid sign of the Jolly Huntsman was brilliantly illuminated; and as soon as he opened the door and went inside (stooping a trifle, for he was a tall man) Hooky knew that he had come in the right sort of place.

The ceiling was low; the woodwork everywhere was dark with age and polished by generations of care; at the far end of the room a small intensely hot fire made nonsense of the chilliness in the evening air; above the bar hung a whole ar-ray of pewter tankards; behind the bar in place of the Junoesque creature with buxom bosom and answering eye who would have been perfect in the part stood a short, rather tubby, extremely dignified gentleman whose silver hairs and courtly manners would have done credit to an archdeacon.

The evening was still young and evidently the drinking fraternity of Exdale had not yet started operations, for only one other customer was in the bar when Hooky went in, a man in a sporting tweed jacket and corduroy trousers standing at the far end.

The walls were hung with a whole range of photographs of various hearty local gentlemen engaged in the noble sport of pursuing, cornering and killing harmless deer.

The Archdeacon subjected Hooky to an unobtrusive, as-sessing scrutiny. . . not one of his regulars; a stranger; hab-its and requirements therefore unknown. . . .

'Good evening, sir,' he said.

The entirely congenial atmosphere of the place was already permeating Hooky's spirit and he returned the greeting enthusiastically.

'I haven't been in a pub for a week,' he declared. 'It's like coming home.'

> 'Whoe'er has travell'd life's dull round,
>   Whate'er his stages may have been,
>   May sigh to think he still has found
>   The warmest welcome at an inn'

the Archdeacon said. 'William Shenstone 1714 to 1763. Only a minor poet certainly, but those four lines have always appealed to me. Particularly since I took up the profession of innkeeper.'

'You haven't always been an innkeeper, then?' Hooky enquired.

'Not always, sir. No. What do you fancy?'

During the poetic interlude Hooky had caught the eye of the other customer and had been treated to an expressive wink; the wink conspiratorial and the information which said *Don't be surprised or alarmed. The old boy isn't off his rocker, only a bit of a character; but he knows his stuff all right. You've come to a good spot.*

'What would really restore my faith in life, which has been flagging lately,' said Hooky, 'is a large cold Pimms Number One. Can you manage that?'

'Certainly, sir,' the Archdeacon said. 'Excuse me one moment whilst I assemble the necessary ingredients.' He disappeared behind a red curtain hanging over a doorway at the back of the bar and Hooky said to the man who had winked at him. 'Unusual sort of pub-keeper, isn't he?'

'Decidedly. But there's nothing wrong with what he serves or the way he serves it. He's quite famous in these parts apparently.'

'You're not a local, then?'

'I've only been here a few months. You've got to live here for ten years at least before you cease to be a foreigner. Are you on holiday?'

'You might put it that way. I'm trying to write a book.'

'Good Lord. Forgive my sounding surprised but I should never have guessed you to be an author. You don't look the literary type to me.'

'I don't look the writing type to myself, much,' Hooky had to confess, 'but still, I bash away at it.'

The first Pimms was succeeded by a second in case, as Hooky explained, the first one should feel lonely; and then, because Hooky was a great believer in lucky numbers and no one could deny the potency of three, a third one was ordered.

Various people drifted in and out; eventually the stranger in the tweed jacket and corduroys finished his final drink, said a courteous 'good night' and went out.

'Seems an amiable sort of chap,' Hooky said to the Archdeacon. 'One of your regulars?'

'Fairly regular, sir. Captain Berry by name. He doesn't live here in Exdale. Some little distance out on the moor, I understand, a house called Castlecroft. They haven't been there long. Mrs Berry goes in for riding quite a bit—well, nearly everybody does on the moor—and the local gossip is that he is going to take up bees or some such hobby.'

'Captain did you say? A bit young to retire, isn't he?'

The Archdeacon smiled. 'I'm afraid that with advancing years everybody else begins to seem a bit young, sir. That's the way of life.'

'You're a philosopher. What was that bit you started off with from Billy Shenstone about the warmest welcome at an inn?'

'Ah, I'm glad that appealed to you, sir. I thought it might. It could be paralleled, perhaps ever bettered, by a quotation from the great doctor: ''There is nothing which has yet been contrived by man by which so much happiness is produced as by a good tavern or inn."'

'You can say that again,' Hooky agreed heartily. 'Who produced that gem?'

'Doctor Samuel Johnson, the lexicographer, 1709 to 1784.'

'Bully for Sam. I must remember to tell the boys in El Vino that one.'

'You frequent Fleet Street, sir?'

'I have done. More than a bit. In my green and salad days.'

'I'm afraid you'll find it rather quiet down here on the moor, sir,' the Archdeacon said.

Hooky laughed. 'You might not think it,' he said, 'but I'm a quiet sort of fellow. Quiet down here on the moor? How else shall I write my masterpiece? I hope it will be quiet. Quietness suits me.'

He took his leave feeling in great good humour after such a pleasant evening and blissfully unaware of how little peace and quiet the moor was going to allow him.

FIVE

CLOSING THE DOOR of the warm and friendly Huntsman behind him Captain Berry climbed into his parked Land Rover and set off along the lonely and by now well-known road over the moor to Castlecroft.

The few lights of the little town were soon left behind and all round him there was nothing but the darkness and the solitude of the moor.

Castlecroft was even more remote—if such a thing were possible—than Sheepsgate, and Edward Baillie-Wilson (Berry was a nickname which it had been convenient to assume permanently) was glad that his stay there would be a limited one.

He had already been there four months ('We'll do this properly,' Big Boy had said. 'Take our time. No hurry. What's a week or two compared to twenty-five years? Get yourself properly established down there; accepted; eccentric country gent, retired Army Wallah—you can play that part all right. Just fit in. Quietly. Don't attract any attention. Normal. When you've got yourself a niche there I'll lay things on.').

Berry hummed happily to himself on the way home. It had been a pleasant, uneventful evening. He was quite prepared to take part in events that were neither pleasant or uneventful, but he could enjoy a quiet drink in a sleepy country pub as well as anybody.

A light mist was beginning to form over the moor by the time he reached Castlecroft and the night had turned colder. He was glad to get indoors.

The woman he was living with—'Mrs Berry' as far as the neighbourhood knew—was sitting on a low stool in front of a splendid fire. She wore a scarlet polo-necked jumper and slacks. She was good-looking in a hard, almost masculine way.

When Berry came in she turned her head and held up her glass in a welcoming gesture.

'The country's pretty damned awful in a lot of ways,' she said, 'but, by God, when we get back to London I'll miss these marvellous fires. Imagine two bars of electricity, at reduced voltage most likely, compared to this.'

Berry helped himself to a drink from a corner cupboard and came to sit beside her.

She was not his wife, but that was in total accord with the character of the man. He belonged essentially to the modern, rootless world. The word 'loyalty' made him laugh uncomprehendingly.... Loyalty to what? Class? Religion? Some established order of things? As far as he was concerned these things didn't exist. What little bit of history he had read (and he was an intelligent man) told him that 1914 had killed them and the years after 1945 had buried them. For Edward Berry there were no loyalties and no ties. There was the business of living and getting as much out of it by way of excitement and money as you could.

He had gone to the same public school which three generations of Baillie-Wilsons had attended before him. All of them had carved their names in the traditional place before leaving; he hadn't bothered to.

From school he had straightway enlisted as a private in a Guards regiment. He was physically fit and tough and didn't mind—in fact for a time rather enjoyed—the harshness of the life.

After three years, instead of pursuing the possibility of going in for the commission which was offered him, he came out of the Army and attached himself to the fringes of the entertainment world in the West End.

He was well built and of good looks and he had vague hopes of doing something in the world of films or the theatre.

Ultimately, and almost accidentally, he found himself running a so-called 'club' in Baker Street. 'Club' was really a polite fiction, because all anybody needed to get into the place was enough money to pay the somewhat exorbitant charges. There was nothing particularly sinister about the place and not even anything outrageously illegal. You could eat and drink there at all hours (there was more drinking than eating); you could gamble if you wanted to (roulette and chemmy); you could retire with your partner to one of the three small 'private rooms' (but this cost a good deal extra); occasionally drugs changed hands there. All this happened, but by and large the One-O-One was not a place the police worried about particularly; they had many spots of a more troublesome nature to keep them busy. Which was almost certainly why the man known as Big Boy began to frequent it.

He must have had a name and at one time in his life presumably he was known by it; but not now. Nowadays nobody ever referred to him as anything other than 'Big Boy'.

He was middle-aged; prematurely middle-aged, because in years he was not yet fifty, but the hair was already thinning off the prominent forehead, the belly already full and sagging. He had a very slight lisp and a disconcerting trick of staring at you with eyes that never seemed to blink. His hands were podgy and his white puffy fingers beringed. He was known to be very rich; his riches came from an empire based on lust and greed and fear and violence.

He was a power in the underworld and men were afraid of him.

Whether by accident or design he first visited the One-O-One is immaterial. Visit it he did, and the place appealed to him. It was away from his usual haunts and not frequented by the usual gangs.

On that first visit he had, of course, two henchmen with him. Like other prime ministers and heads of state Big Boy didn't travel anywhere without strong-arm protection.

Berry, then, had no idea who his visitor was and at the end of the evening presented the very considerable bill—dinner for three and two bottles of champagne—in the usual way.

Without bothering to look at the amount one of the strong-arm men, delighted by the chance of shewing his chief how useful he was, tore the bill in half and threw the pieces on to the floor.

'Get wise, bud,' he advised. 'Big Boy doesn't pay bills.'

Flummoxed for the moment Berry stared at him.

The henchman laughed at his naïve bewilderment. 'You want this joint to stay put-together, bud? O.K. No bills, no trouble. That's the way of it.'

Big Boy, who was in an amiable mood that evening, liked the appearance of the well-built useful-looking proprietor; he signalled to him to sit down.

After that Big Boy came to the One-O-One fairly frequently. The place suited him and he had taken a fancy to Berry. Not only had he taken a fancy to him but he had noted him as being of possible use in some future contingency. He had earmarked Berry as a gentleman by birth, a man with army training and a natural law-breaker; and Big Boy thought that this combination of assets might prove useful one day.

That day came when the big bank-raid in Croydon High Street went wrong.

Big Boy had set the raid up himself, so everyone in the underworld believed; and his particular friend Lenny 'Three Fingers' Dawson was to carry it out.

One hundred and eighty thousand pounds were there for what, after so much careful planning, seemed easy taking. But for once the careful planning went awry and things miscarried.

A civilian onlooker who had no right to be so public-spirited intervened and got shot for his pains; but his intervention fouled up the enterprise, which ended with one security man dead, one civilian injured, no hundred and eighty thousand pounds in the bag, and Lenny Dawson together with his two associates in custody.

Big Boy didn't mind much about the two associates; he regarded them as expendable; but he didn't like Lenny being taken. Lenny was his own particular pal; Lenny was near to him.

A lot of people in the underworld thought that Big Boy was a homo and that Lenny was, or had been, one of his 'friends'.

It could well have been so. There was a lot about Big Boy that nobody knew. But after the Croydon fiasco, and when the judge sent Lenny down for twenty-five years, one thing was certain—Big Boy was determined to get him out.

Whether it was sentiment, or pride, or whatever the motive, Big Boy staked his reputation on getting Lenny Dawson out of Dartmoor.

The underworld knew this and the underworld watched to see how, and indeed if, it could be done.

Big Boy began deliberately and methodically to put together his plan; the time to make use of the tough-looking proprietor of the One-O-One had come.

At Castlecroft the silence was interrupted by the ringing of the telephone and Berry went into the hall to answer it. He was out of the room for some time and when he came back the woman looked at him enquiringly.

'Big Boy?'

He nodded. 'Yes. It's to be Tuesday the fourteenth.'

'Tuesday the fourteenth? Couldn't suit better. There's a show just outside Exeter and if anyone stops me on the way back I can say I've been there.'

'Good. Maybe that's a sign that the whole thing will be lucky. I think signs and portents and omens are a lot of

damned rot, but I believe in them all the same. Get the two-
and-a-half-inch ordnance map and let's go over the scheme
once again.'

The map was spread out on a low table, the drinks were
recharged and another log thrown on the fire. The woman
lit a cigarette, inhaled and threw out a long thin plume of
smoke.

'I suppose it's quite certain that Lenny Dawson will be out
working on Tuesday the fourteenth?' she said.

'I think you can trust Big Boy to get that right. Of course
it does depend on the weather; if there's a mist they won't
send working parties out. Apart from that, yes, it's certain.
There's this screw inside who knows the rota of people
working and Lenny will be out on that Tuesday.'

'If Big Boy has got this screw in his pay, why can't the
screw get Lenny free?'

'Talk sense, Betty. It's damned difficult for a screw to let
a prisoner get free and not be charged with neglect of duty.
Impossible probably. Neglect of duty and connivance. It
would be worth five years at the least and no chance of a job
when the poor sod came out. No screw is going to risk that.
But to say the two words "Tuesday" and "Farthinghoe"
and get fifty quid for it. What risk is there in that? Now
where's the map?

'It's to be Tuesday the fourteenth and Farthinghoe
Quarry. Here we are, *here*. That's where the working party
will be. I did a recce there last week. The whole point is
about the tools. They don't bring the picks and shovels out
with them any more; they reckoned it would be better security not to have a busload of men each carrying something that could be a very useful weapon, so they come out
with nothing and the tools are waiting for them on the spot.

'This quarry isn't much of a place; it's not particularly
deep. At the bottom of it, tucked away under an overhang-
ing chunk of rock, there's the hut. Did you ever see one of
the Anderson air-raid shelters they dished out in the last

war? Well, it's very much like one of those. The picks and shovels are kept in there. When the working party arrives the screw in charge unlocks the hut and the prisoners go in one at a time to get what they are told to get—pick or shovel as the case may be. When they are all out, and counted just to make sure, the hut is locked up again and they start work. When it's knocking-off time they do the whole thing in reverse: one at a time; in; put your pick or shovel away; out again; lock up; count again, into the bus and back to the prison.

'The hut is what I suppose the authorities would call "securely padlocked". It looks formidable enough, but of course formidable-looking padlocks don't mean much to Big Boy, and I've got a key that opens it.

'Inside the hut there's a row of picks and shovels all neatly stacked and some bits of sacking on the floor. Nothing else—yet.

'As we've been told the zero hour—Tuesday the fourteenth—I shall have to get busy on the Monday night.

'I shall have to have the motor-cycle and the twenty pounds of gellymix in the Land Rover—'

'Christ, I hate that stuff, Teddy,' the woman said. 'I know it's silly, but I just don't like bombs.'

Berry grinned. 'Who does like 'em?' he answered. 'Particularly if you happen to be next to one when it goes off. But don't worry; you won't have anything to do with it.'

'Suppose somebody stops you on Monday night and searches the Land Rover?'

'Be your age, Betty. *If, if, if* somebody finds a gellymix bomb inside a Land Rover in the middle of Dartmoor they are going to ask questions, aren't they? But, in Heaven's name, two o'clock in the morning, a bit of a wild night with any luck, who's going to be about to stop me and ask questions?

'I shan't be more than five minutes anyway. Scarcely that. All I've got to do is to hide the gellymix bomb among the sacking on the floor of the hut and get the Norton stowed away—'

'Have you got a place earmarked for that?'

'Yes, there's a clump of bushes, scrubby thorny stuff, on the edge of the quarry, just in the best possible position and with quite enough cover to hide the motor-bike.'

The woman nodded. 'You always make everything sound easy, Teddy. I expect it will be all right.'

'It will go like clockwork. And incidentally that's one benefit of being up against people like prison authorities—they work—they've got to work—according to rules and timetables, which is a great help in making one's plans.

'What's going to happen is this: The working party will de-bus at the Quarry at two o'clock Tuesday. Might be five minutes out one way or the other, but you can call it two near enough.

'"Right, out with you, get lined up, be counted, and let's have you"—the usual N.C.O. stuff.

'Then they'll go into the hut, one at a time, to get their picks and shovels.

'Lenny's going to fix things so that he goes in last and then all he's got to do is to bend down quickly, pull the sacking to one side, turn the fuse on the gellymix to five, pull the sacking back over it, grab his shovel or whatever and out.

'In five minutes' time the bomb will go off.

'Of course we can't be certain exactly where Lenny will be at that precise moment, but he certainly won't be far away from the bushes where the Norton will be hidden; and, with a bit of luck and skilful management, he might be very close to them.'

'And what happens exactly when the bomb goes off?'

Berry laughed. 'One hell of a bang happens,' he said. 'Believe me, gellymix is powerful stuff; when twenty pounds of it is touched off there will be the very devil of a mess. That hut will be blown to glory. There'll be chunks of timber and lumps of rock and clods of earth flying all over the place. It's one thing to read about a bomb explosion happening, it's quite another thing to be there at the time. You can take it from me that for a couple of minutes, at least, nobody will have grasped what the hell has happened.

'Nobody except Lenny, that is.

'That's the critical part of the whole plan. The two minutes' confusion that the explosion is bound to cause. If Lenny doesn't get away then, he never will. I think it's at least an even chance that he will. Yes, I reckon any self-respecting bookie would make it even money. Fifty-fifty.

'Lenny has got to break and run for it. And never mind the screws and their whistles and carbines.

'If he can get to the bushes, drag the Norton out and be away on it, he'll stand a very big chance.'

'And you think he will be able to?'

'Like I say, fifty-fifty. In my opinion it's certainly no worse than an even chance. And anyway Big Boy thinks it's worth trying and so we're going to try it.

'If he doesn't make the bushes and get away the thing's a non-starter and maybe Big Boy will think of something else. That's up to him. And in any case Lenny can't be much worse off. There'll be no possible way of connecting him personally with the bomb, and as he's in for twenty-five years anyway there's not much more they can do to him.

'We've got to go on the assumption that he will get away, that there will be enough confusion in those first two or three minutes for him to reach the Norton and be off on it.

'If that happens (and I'm optimistic enough to think that it will) of course the screws will get into a frightful tizzy; they'll be blowing their whistles and shouting "One away" and using their pocket radios for all they're worth.

'The classic thing, the regulation thing (and the regulations *are* the classics for these people) is to set up road blocks. You read it in the papers every time, don't you: "This afternoon a prisoner escaped from a working party at Dartmoor and road blocks were immediately set up on all the moorland roads."

'It sounds all right; but the weak point about it from the prison authorities' point of view is that one word "immediately".

'In point of fact you can't set up road blocks "immediately". There's quite a deal of machinery to be put in motion. You've got to send out the appropriate messages saying what's happened to start with; then you've got to get your men together, calling some of them in from other duties, and they have to make their way out to the traditional spots and get the actual blocks into position.

'So what does "immediately" mean? I don't believe it can possibly mean less than sixty minutes, an hour. And a man in a hurry can travel a long way on a seven-horsepower Norton in an hour.

'But, of course, Lenny doesn't have to travel all that distance. That isn't the plan.

'And this is where you come into it.

'Big Boy reckons the timing, as near as we can estimate it, will be like this:

—Work party arrive at the Quarry at 2 p.m.

—De-bus, usual formalities, start to get tools.

—Bomb goes of 2.10 (within a minute or so).

—Lenny starts away on the Norton, say, 2.13. This may be 2.13, 2.14, 2.15, it doesn't matter really; the point is that he'll be at the rendezvous approximately twenty minutes later so you've got to be ready for him any time from 2.25 onwards.

'Now, you've got this rendezvous absolutely fixed in your head, haven't you?'

The woman nodded, 'Yes, absolutely.'

'Let's check it on the map. Buckfastleigh, here we are. The A384 running south-east from it. Not all that much traffic on it when I've checked, and anyway you won't be waiting on the main road itself. A mile and a half after the

Buckfastleigh turn there's an old green lane—it's marked on the map, here—'

'I know it perfectly well. You've shewn it to me.'

'Well, that's the place. Have the horse box there, with the pony in it and the gear for Lenny and the back open. Just out of sight of the road. As soon as Lenny appears get him and the Norton into the box as quickly as you can. Up with the back and away you start for home on the roundabout route we worked out.

'You ought to be away just after two-thirty. Then make a big half-circle of it, Exeter, Crediton and back that way.

'I don't believe for one moment that anyone will be stopping traffic as far afield as that.'

Betty nodded. She was beginning to be excited by the idea of taking part in the escape.

'No, neither do I,' she agreed. 'I ought to have him back here by about four-thirty, I should think.'

'Just in time for tea,' Berry grinned, 'and once we have got him here we know where to hide him. All that's fixed. And then, of course, the other part of Big Boy's plan comes into operation. At a quarter to three a man rides into the station car-park at Exeter on a white Norton, the dead image of the one Lenny got away on. He leaves the bike there and fades away.

'Although the screws in charge of the working party are going to be flummoxed for a minute or two when the bomb goes off, at least one of them will get some sort of view of Lenny making off on the Norton. They might even spot the make; they are certain to spot that it's an all-white solo machine. In due course—probably twenty-four hours—Exeter police will report an all-white Norton apparently abandoned in the car-park of Exeter Station and the Law will come to the conclusion that Lenny made it to Exeter, caught the London train and is hiding in the Smoke.'

'And how long have we got to keep him hidden here?'

'Until we hear from Big Boy. He'll work that out. It doesn't matter how long it is. After all, we are fifty miles away from Dartmoor here. No one will have the slightest reason for suspecting us of anything. When Big Boy gives the "all clear" Lenny will go; and so shall we. We'll cease being retired country gentry, pick up our five thousand from Big Boy and go and live it up in the sunshine somewhere.'

SIX

FENELLA WAS DUE at the flower shop in the Burlington Arcade at a quarter to nine each morning. She was never late. It was in her nature to like things done tidily and neatly; and 'tidily and neatly' meant, amongst other things, being punctual.

Ruth, on the other hand, was hardly ever punctual. Ruth was Colin's other assistant and was as unlike Fenella as could possibly be imagined.

Colin, who owned the shop, called them 'the elegant' and 'the earthy'.

Good-hearted, straightforward Ruth took not the slightest offence at being called 'earthy'; and she was the very first to admit that Fenella deserved to be known as 'elegant'. Ruth's upbringing, background and the general ambience of her life were very different from Fenella's, but she was possessed of two outstanding characteristics: she had a natural genius for flower arrangement (Fenella was good at it but Ruth was brilliant) and an equally natural genius for sex.

She wasn't particularly good-looking, she wasn't particularly smart, but there was something elemental about her which was strongly stimulating to the masculine urge and which responded to it with cheerful abandon.

Most of Ruth's conversation in the shop every morning consisted of an enthusiastic account of her adventures of the evening, and generally of the night, before. It was very naïve, and in spite of the alarmingly frank nature of many of her reminiscences it managed to have a curious air of innocence about it all.

Fenella found it highly entertaining; and, moved by Ruth's obvious expectancy of something colourful in return, she occasionally felt constrained to invent a few experiences of her own.

Ruth listened to these eagerly; but whether she really believed them is doubtful. She had by now become accustomed to the extraordinary fact that Fenella was still a virgin.

'Never mind,' she used to say consolingly when animadverting to this strange phenomenon. 'Just you wait, Fen, some day....'

'What sort of party was it?' Ruth asked, reminiscing a few days after the rout at Chessington Gardens.

'Oh, the usual sort of thing: lots of people, lots to eat and drink if you wanted it.'

'It was at the Townsends', wasn't it?'

'That's right, yes.'

'But their parties are *famous*, Fen. They get written up in the papers, don't they?'

'In the gossip columns occasionally, yes.'

'And you went all *alone*?'

'Actually I don't mind that. I knew lots of people there anyway.'

'Fen, I could *shake* you. You, with all your marvellous looks and everything. My God, I wish I had a figure like yours. Do you mean to tell me there wasn't anybody *special*? *Fen!* I do believe you're blushing! There *was* somebody special; there must have been. How marvellous! Do tell me.'

Fenella laughed; it was impossible to take any sort of offence at Ruth's enthusiasms.

'There was somebody who was described as a soldier of fortune,' she allowed.

'What a splendid phrase. Good-looking?'

'In a rugged sort of way.'

'Tall?'

'He looked a bit like a rugby forward.'

Ruth rolled her brown eyes heavenward. 'Bliss,' she said. 'And did you—I mean, you *got together*, didn't you?'

'Mildly.'

'Oh my God, Fen, mildly! What on earth is that supposed to mean? What's the good of getting together mildly? It's either fireworks or nothing. What happened anyway?'

'I sent him away.'

'You sent him away?'

'In a manner of speaking, yes. I got him a job in the country.'

'Well, that's not too bad. You can go down and visit him. You'll probably have him to yourself in the wilds of wherever he is.'

'But I don't know where he is, Ruth.'

Ruth stared at her incredulously.

'My God,' she said at length. 'You really are a poor specimen of the Seducers' Union. You ought to be drummed out of the regiment of women. A great big heavenly specimen of a he-man falls into your lap and you pack him off on a job somewhere and don't even know where it is! Honestly, Fen, you want your head examined.'

Fenella laughed again, but for once in a way Ruth's comments stung a little. During the day she reflected more than once on them. When shutting-up time came she was the last to leave the shop (as she frequently was) and her final act, all formalities being completed, was to reach for the telephone.

She had seen nothing of Charles Wilbury lately, the man of law having been even busier than usual, and in fact he was on the very point of leaving Lincoln's Inn Fields when her call came.

'Charles, you are an elusive person.'

'I've been frightfully busy, Fen; rushed off my feet. What can I do for you?'

'Good God, Charles, I'm not one of your clients.'

'No, no. Of course not. I'm sorry. I mean how nice to hear from you.'

'I'm thirsty, Charles. I'm inviting myself to a drink. Will you be in at half past sixish?'

'This evening?'

'This very evening.'

She was conscious of, and annoyed by, the slightest of slight pauses; then—

'Yes, rather. That's a splendid idea. I'm on my way up to Hampstead now with a document for signature, but I'll be home before six. By six-thirty certainly. Yes, do come. Fen; it will be delightful to see you.'

Just to be on the safe side, and knowing what the man of law was once he got entangled with documents of any sort, Fenella timed her arrival at Timmerton Square for seven o'clock.

She walked into the warm, comfortable, civilized drawing-room of Charles's flat, with the elegant French furniture and the two Delagasses, one on either side of the fireplace.

Charles had said that it would be delightful to see her; but somehow Fenella didn't get much impression of delight. Politeness, of course; Charles would never be anything but polite; perhaps that's the trouble, Fenella thought, and she wondered, with some inward amusement, how earthy Ruth would fare with him.

More than ever the man of law seemed very well pleased with himself, a ripe purveyor of Puffed-up Platitudes from Peacock Lane, Fenella thought, surveying him with some amusement.

'You got your document signed all right up at Hampstead?' she asked.

'Oh Lord, yes. These big men tend to keep one on the run a bit, but in the end one can usually get them to see sense. May I get you a drink, Fenella?'

'A vodka and lime. I've really come for some information, Charles....'

The man of law looked slightly startled. Possibly he was too busy to want another client; possibly he didn't think Fenella could afford the sort of fee that he liked to charge.

'Well, naturally, anything I can do...' he said somewhat warily.

'I've been expecting a big vote of thanks.'

'A vote of thanks? Sorry, you're losing me—'

'That day you took me to lunch at the Ecu, weren't you desperately anxious to get hold of a suitable companion-tutor type for the supposedly vulnerable son of that disgustingly rich man up in Hampstead?'

Charles was slightly dismayed at hearing his valued client referred to in these terms, and he reflected that women, even the best of them, have very little sense of proportion.

'Yes, I was.'

'And didn't I provide you with one? Straight off the cuff and out of the hat?'

'Indeed you did, Fenella; indeed you did. A marvellous bit of luck your having just the sort of person I was looking for. I went round straight away to see him. You've been to his—well, I don't know whether to call it an office or not—to where he lives anyway?'

Fenella shook her head.

'One couldn't call it impressive exactly. I must say Soho has become a pretty tawdry place these days; but the man himself, Hefferman, he's turned out to be absolutely all right, just what one was looking for.'

'Didn't I tell you he would be? He's a soldier of fortune.'

Charles nodded approvingly. 'An apt description, I would think. Loeson was delighted that I got the whole thing fixed up for him so quickly. So you definitely get your vote of thanks. Very much so.'

'And where is the soldier of fortune now?'

'Where is he?'

'That's what I want to know, Charles; that's the piece of information I came for.'

'He's looking after Loeson's boy.'

'That's what he is doing; what I want to know is where is he doing it?'

Charles turned to the drinks table and refreshed his glass. Facing the room, and Fenella, again he began to set up his defences.

He smiled his most amiable smile.

'Well, let us say it is in the country,' he countered.

'I'm sure it's in the country,' Fenella replied a trifle sharply (in point of fact she remembered Charles's own reference to his cousin 'away down in the West Country'), 'but where?'

'I'm very sorry, Fenella, but I can't tell you.'

She stared at him unbelievingly.

'Come off it, Charles; don't put on the cautious lawyer act with me. I want to get in touch with the soldier of fortune. Damn it all, I got him the job and I'm curious to know how he's making out in it.'

'I can assure you that everything is going along very well indeed.'

'I don't want to hear that from you. I want to hear it from him.'

'I'm sorry, Fenella, I cannot tell you the address.'

'But this is ludicrous, and incidentally something of an insult—'

'I'm sorry if you think that.'

'Of course I think it. You don't suppose I intend to do this wretched boy any harm, do you?'

'Of course not.'

'Very well, then, tell me where he is tucked away.'

'I can't do that.'

'What you're saying is that you don't trust me.'

'My dear girl—'

'I wish you would not use that fat, smooth, smug, ego-tistical, masculine phrase when talking to me. It annoys me intensely.'

'I'm sorry. I had no idea you felt like that.'

'And don't keep saying "I'm sorry", Charles. All I want you to do is to tell me the address where Hooky Hefferman is doing the job which, after all, I got for him.'

Charles Wilbury didn't want to stick to his principles and in so doing annoy the girl in whom he was allowing himself to be interested and there was something rather dignified, heroic even, about his high-mindedness in the matter.

'I am sure you will realize,' he said, 'that the one thing a solicitor mustn't, *can't*, do is to betray the confidence of a client. It's like these R.C. priests and confession. If the client tells you something and says "This is private; I don't want anybody else to know about it" you simply cannot divulge it.'

'I don't think you would make a very good R.C. priest, Charles.'

'I'm sure I wouldn't. Much too fond of the flesh-pots. But I'd be all right on the seal-of-confession business. Now, may I get you another drink?'

'Mollify the tiresome female with alcohol—is that the idea?'

Charles smiled. The heat seemed to be going out of the situation. 'Partly,' he admitted.

'Fair enough.' Fenella extended her glass. 'Plenty of ice this time.'

'I'll get some more,' Charles said and went out of the room to do so.

Fenella was almost as much amused as annoyed. She had not expected such an excess of professional integrity on Charles Wilbury's part. Secretly she had to admit that she was impressed by it. She wondered if earthy Ruth with her more primitive approach would have succeeded in getting what she wanted.

She moved idly across the room. The two Delagasses were familiar but she had spotted something new hanging over the desk at the far end.

It was a small coloured print of the interior of Prinny's arabesque riding-school in Brighton, the architectural setting being drawn by Pugin, the figures by Rowlandson. Altogether a delicate and delightful little thing. The man of law might be tiresome in many ways, she reflected, but he had good taste.

Her eye fell from the lively little print to the desk over which it hung. A desk characteristically neat and tidy. An amusing stone frog as a guardian on top of a pile of what with most people would be bills but in Charles Wilbury's case, she felt certain, must be receipts. A sumptuously bound 'Engagement Book' occupied pride of place in the centre of things and close to it a memorandum pad.

On the memorandum pad was written something which Fenella didn't, at first, consciously read; it was simply that her eyes saw the black marks on the white paper and mechanically registered them: 'Exdale 291'.

When her host came back with the ice Fenella was in the centre of the room.

'Sorry to have been so long. My fridge has got what I can only describe as a very reluctant ice-compartment; it's very difficult to get anything out of it.'

'Rather like its owner. Not to worry. I've been admiring your pictures.'

It was quite true that she had been admiring the little coloured print; it was also true that the one scribbled note 'Exdale 291' had started a train of thought in her lively mind.... 'Tucked away in the West Country,' Charles had said in an unguarded moment and now there was this telephone number 'Exdale 291'.

Fenella knew Exdale; she had friends living there; if any

phrase deserved the description 'tucked away in the West Country', surely little Exdale did.

Fenella, always willing for an adventure, didn't see why she shouldn't go in for a little private-eye business on her own.

SEVEN

DUSTER IN HAND HOOKY STEPPED back to get a better view of the beautiful polish he was putting on the ancient body-work of his beloved car. In London the Jag didn't get the attention it deserved; Hooky would have been the first to acknowledge that fact and the first to feel contrite about it; but down at Sheepsgate it was different. At Sheepsgate time seemed to be a different substance altogether from the hectic stuff of which there was never enough up in London; here, with the silence of the moor and the simplicity of little things around you, there was plenty of time to do everything; time to sit and stare at the blank page that you ought to be filling with amusing reminiscences from your sometimes lurid past; time to get tired of that and to borrow some rags and a duster from your hostess and go out to give a beauty treatment to the Jag.

Hooky put his head on one side and considered his handiwork; to him it looked good; he congratulated himself on a splendid job.

'Not bad,' said a deflating and condescending voice behind him.

A pained expression passed over Hooky's face. There were times when he doubted his sanity at having taken on this nursemaid-to-a-prize-pest assignment.

'I wish you would let me drive it,' Simon said complainingly.

This was not the first time the request had been made and Hooky was delighted at the chance of saying 'no' once again and with emphasis.

'Not a chance, sonny; not one small minute chance in the whole of hell.'

'But I can drive perfectly well. I understand the theory of the internal combustion engine absolutely.'

'I'm sure you do. I'm sure you are one of these Young Scientist of the Year characters. I'm sure you know all about radio-active isotopes and the square root of your grandmother's backside minus one. I'm sure scientific knowledge is running out of your ears. But you don't drive my Jag. For one thing, you're too young to have a licence and you aren't insured.'

'There wouldn't be the slightest danger round here. We never see anybody all day.'

'Forget it.'

'I'm afraid you have an exaggerated respect for conventional things, Hooky, for the Law and all that.'

'Quite right, sonny. When the Law happens to be on my side I have the very greatest respect for it, so belt up.'

'Pity. Of course, it's an extremely inefficient way of generating power.'

'What is?'

'The internal combustion engine. A thing like your old crock here. It's ludicrously wasteful. Only about eight per cent of the force generated in the cylinders ultimately gets through to the road wheels. I can prove it to you in a diagram if you like.'

'For God's sake—'

'All right, all right. I quite realize that your generation doesn't want to be shewn facts. We all realize that.'

'Who's "we all"?'

'People of my age. The coming generation.'

'You know the lot, of course, don't you?'

'I think we probably do.'

'My God, what modesty.'

'I don't see the point of being modest. You never get anywhere like that.'

Hooky laughed. He had to admit that in the course of a picturesque career modesty had not always been his own outstanding characteristic. Occasionally he found Simon intensely irritating, but there was no point in losing his temper with the boy.

'Take a tip from me, Simon boy,' he said amiably. 'Don't be so damned serious. Don't try to know everything about everything. It just isn't on. Life isn't lived like that. Take it easy for a bit. What's wrong with being down here anyway? We're on holiday. Let's enjoy ourselves.'

'If we are on holiday, why can't I ride Cinders?'

'You're an obstinate little so-and-so, aren't you? We've had all this out half a dozen times already. You can't ride Cinders, and I can't ride Cinders and even Francis can't ride Cinders because Rachel says we can't. She owns the horse and she says no one is to ride it but herself.'

'You believe in the concept of private property?'

'Don't start being a starry-eyed young Marxist with me, my boy. I believe in having your own bit of everything and hanging on to it.'

'No wonder the world's in such a mess. How's that book of yours coming along?'

'Slowly.'

'You don't really do much at it, do you?'

'Writing a book is very hard work. You can take that from me.'

'And there isn't much money in it, is there? Personally I don't see the point of slaving away at a thing unless you are going to make money out of it. I believe in making a lot of money. As far as I can see, most people of your generation don't understand about money. Now, I've got a theory about it—'

'Listen, sonny,' Hooky cut in, speaking in a restrained, but firm, voice. 'You are just about the biggest bloody nuisance in the whole wide world; but you are also, or you should be at your tender age, innocent and uncorrupted; so, although I have very strong views as to what you could do with your wonderful theory about money, I shall refrain, by heroic self-restraint, from detailing it to you. Now beggar off.'

Hooky had come to accept these semi-amusing, semi-irritating brushes with the boy as inseparable from the job he had undertaken; and on the whole he was managing to survive them pretty well. Abrasive conversations with Simon were, after all, only a part of an existence which had much to commend it. There was a quality about life as it was lived at Sheepsgate which began to impress itself upon him. In the evening, after Simon had gone up to bed, there was something very agreeable about sitting with his host and hostess before the dying remains of a huge log-fire and in the soft radiance of an oil-lamp.

Talk would be intermittent and undemanding; the silence of the moor, which somehow crept into the house and pervaded it, seemed too precious a thing to disturb unnecessarily.

There was no T.V. 'Some of our friends tell me we ought to have one,' Francis said in his quiet way, 'but we've escaped so far.' An old-fashioned radio set did exist, but it was seldom turned on. One evening, when by some whim or other it did get switched on, Hooky listened with growing astonishment to three highly verbose individuals all discussing away at nineteen to the dozen about, as far as could be ascertained, nothing at all.

It was such self-satisfied, repetitive, convoluted nonsense that Hooky could not imagine how he had ever thought listening worth while, let alone important.

From his point of view the most important and gratifying fact about being at Sheepsgate was the obvious absence of any danger to his charge.

He never had thought the kidnapping business was anything but a figment of Loeson's extremely active and apprehensive Jewish imagination; and since nobody could possibly know where the boy Simon had been taken to Hooky felt safe in concluding that the question of risk to him did not in fact exist.

There remained the problem of keeping him reasonably occupied and contented during each day; and this was proving unexpectedly easy.

Simon attached himself to Francis a good deal and followed his host round the endless sequence of small farming jobs to be seen to about the place, occasionally lending a hand when too much physical exertion was not involved.

When the boy got tired of doing that and felt in need of more positive amusement he would seek out Hooky and goad him into suppressed fury with endless questions and suggestions for leading a more useful and financially rewarding existence.

In the evening it had now become established that Francis and Simon played chess.

'He's a very good player,' Francis told Hooky. 'There's no doubt he is an extremely clever boy. I shall be interested to see what happens to him when he grows up.'

'I'll tell you exactly what will happen to him,' Hooky volunteered. 'He'll become one of the most respected figures in that pillar of English probity and integrity, the City. High-class finance and other swindles. Whilst you and I are being chivvied by the income-tax narks because we haven't paid our first instalment yet, he'll be financing a loan to the Arabs to supply them with arms to enable them to provoke an incident which will give Israel an excuse to launch an all-out, unannounced attack. And, of course, to do that Israel itself will want some arms and the finance to buy them and, being attacked, the Arabs will have to buy more arms to defend themselves.'

Francis laughed in his easy, good-natured way.

'You're a cynic, Hooky,' he said, 'which you wouldn't be if you lived down here permanently. Meanwhile Simon is a good chess-player and I am delighted to have him to play against.'

Hooky, too, was delighted that they should play; it allowed him, with a clear conscience, to take an occasional evening off and to renew his acquaintance with the Jolly Huntsman in Exdale.

It was constitutionally impossible for Hooky not to welcome a visit to a pub, but he had to admit that the Jolly Huntsman was not quite coming up to the high expectations which his first acquaintance with it had aroused.

There was nothing wrong with the atmosphere of the place; it looked right, it felt right, it *was* right. The stage, you might say, was perfect; but it lacked a cast. An essential part of any pub in Hooky's philosophy was the noisy, laughing, jostling crowd of lunatics and layabouts through whom you had to elbow your way to get near the bar.

For some psychological reason which Hooky didn't bother even to try to understand (Wiseacre Simon would explain it to me if I ever asked him, he thought grimly) the fact that a whole lot of other people were dishing out money they couldn't afford for the privilege of drinking stuff their stomachs didn't want at the same time as one was doing it oneself made the whole proceeding infinitely more enjoyable.

This agreeable multiplication of lunacy was the one thing lacking in the Huntsman.

Hooky supposed that the place must have its crowded hours of glorious life, but so far he had not struck them. What Hooky wanted in a bar was a crowd, and noise and the sight of *déjà*-bloody-*vu* Duggie propped up against the counter at the far end relating for the nth but still amusing time the one about the bright young lady who thought the vows in the marriage service were 'love, honour and oh baby!'

In the Huntsman he generally found only one solitary local and the courteous purveyor of poetry behind the bar.

But, even so, the snug little inn in the snug little dark street of the snug little dark town was a welcome diversion after a long, quiet day at Sheepsgate, and Hooky continued to go there.

He went there on the evening of the day when he had been cleaning the Jag; the ancient chariot looked resplendent as a result of his efforts, and Hooky parked her with more than usual care in the narrowness of Turnabout Street.

Ahead of him stood a somewhat battered Mini Traveller so it looked as though there might be company of some sort in the bar.

Hooky ducked his head and went through the lower doorway eagerly; the devotee entering the temple.

'Company of some sort' he had half-expected; but not *this* company.

He was so astonished that he stopped in mid-stride and stared.

'Young and dark and lovely,' he had thought her when he first saw her at Freddy Townsend's rout in Chessington Gardens; young and dark and lovely she looked now, standing at the bar, her head tilted back slightly, her eyes dancing with amusement.

'What on earth brings you here?' Hooky demanded.

'The thing said to be lethal to cats,' Fenella told him. 'Curiosity. I wondered how you were getting on.'

Hooky was still staring at her in half-disbelief.

'And how the devil did you know where I was?' he asked. 'Don't tell me you seduced the man of law and wormed the secret out of him?'

'I haven't seduced anybody,' Fenella assured him, 'yet. I did just a little bit of what you would call private-eye work. I took a shot in the dark.'

'Well, you landed bang on target,' Hooky said, grinning delightedly. 'I wonder if the Archdeacon here has a bottle of adequately cold Lanson's Black Label? This calls for a celebration.'

Fenella's 'shot in the dark' had originated from the moment when she had seen 'Exdale 291' on the memorandum pad on Charles Wilbury's desk.

She had gone straight back to her minute flatlet in South Ken and after consulting her address book had dialled another Exdale number. . . .

'*Fenella!* Darling, how lovely to hear your voice. Where are you? Stuck in that frightful London, I suppose. Why on earth don't you come down and see us sometime?'

'That's exactly what I am proposing to do, Angela.'

'How marvellous. Anytime—'

'I thought in a few days. I'm due for a holiday from the flower shop—'

'I'm sure you are. You're much too conscientious, Fen. Conscience gets in the way of everything. Come absolutely any time you like. There's lots to do. The hunter trials next week and the point-to-point as well. Actually I can give you a ride to the Ladies' Race if you would like one.'

So, amid general joy and jubilation, Fen arrived at Fenton Park to take part in the frenzied but amiable confusion of children, horses and dogs which continually reigned there.

On the first evening after Fenella had gone to bed her host and hostess sat discussing her arrival.

'I wonder why she has come here at this precise moment,' Angela mused.

'Wants a holiday, I suppose.'

'Y-e-s. But, I don't know. I can't help feeling—'

'You women have very devious minds.'

'Maybe, maybe. Anyway, it's jolly nice to have her.'

The very next day Fenella had given her private-eye proclivities full rein, enjoying every moment of it.

She toured Exdale.

Going on foot and walking slowly this took about ten minutes. There was only one pub in the place and instinct told her that sooner or later (and sooner rather than later if she were any judge of character) the soldier of fortune would call there for refreshment and sustenance in the battle of life. The Jolly Huntsman was the obvious place.

On her first visit she had instantly charmed the Archdeacon who, being an ex-butler from a titled establishment, reckoned to know the genuine goods when he saw them.

From him she had ascertained beyond any reasonable doubt that the soldier of fortune had indeed become a frequenter of the place.

'Not exactly a regular, miss, but the gentleman you have described does come in occasionally. I understand he is writing a book.'

'So he told me,' said Fenella. 'What it is to be clever!'

'And if I may say so, miss,' the Archdeacon added gallantly, 'the gentleman would appear to be very lucky in his friends.'

Fenella smiled at him (doing Heaven only knows what damage to his ex-butler's heart) as now on her second visit to the Huntsman she smiled at Hooky.

The Archdeacon served the Lanson's Black Label with a flourish.

'I think I could find a few dry biscuits, sir,' he said. 'His Grace was always very partial to a dry biscuit with his glass of champagne.'

Hooky approved. 'What was good enough for His Grace will be good enough for me,' he said.

Over their drinks Fenella explained how she had stumbled across the one word 'Exdale' and had connected it with Charles Wilbury's single unguarded reference in the Ecu to a place 'away down in the West Country'.

'So I thought Exdale worth exploring,' she explained, 'and it was easy to do because I know Angela and Tony Lloyd-Fenton in these parts. Tony's a big wig of some sort hereabouts and they are always asking me to stay at Fenton Park, where in fact I am now, as they say, lodged.'

'I can see I shall have to offer you a job as my assistant,' Hooky said, 'and believe me it's good to see you. The moorland air is a shade too pure and rarefied. I'm nostalgic for a whiff of the old, smoke-laden, vitiated, unbreathable stuff of London Town.'

'It's probably doing you a world of good, Hooky.'

'I'm sure it is; that's one of the most dangerous things about it. I'm not the sort of person to whom good ought to be done.'

'But the job is going all right, is it?'

'In reality there isn't a job. Not for me. That is to say I am more and more convinced that the boy need never have been sent down here. The whole thing is a rich man's nonsense.'

'You don't think the boy is in any danger?'

'At times he is in grave danger—'

Fenella looked surprised and slightly startled.

'He is?' she queried.

'—of getting a clip round the ear. When I get back I'm going to found the S.S.E.P.K., the Society for the Suppression of Egregiously Precocious Kids. But he's not in any danger from outside. Of that I am sure.'

'So there's no reason why you shouldn't take a day off?'

'I expect it could be managed. After all, Francis and Rachel are there all the time.'

'We are thinking of going to the point-to-point in three days' time. It would be nice if I had an escort.'

'You've got one,' Hooky assured her firmly as he replenished their glasses. 'Here's to a fine day and lots of winners.'

EIGHT

AT CASTLECROFT Edward Baillie-Wilson came in by the kitchen door and sat himself at the table in the pleasant expectation of breakfast. He had been out for ten minutes on the moor assessing the probable weather chances of the day, and his appetite, always a good one, had been sharpened by the morning air.

'What's it look like?' Betty asked without turning from the stove where she was busy getting an egg-and-bacon meal together.

'O.K.,' he told her heartily. 'There's probably some country saying about dew in the morning downpour by noon, but to hell with that; country wiseacres are always pessimists anyway. For my money it's going to be a fine and sunny day; no mist or anything; but of course it might be totally different on Dartmoor.'

'We'll put on the local weather forecast at half past,' the woman said. 'One egg or two?'

'Two eggs, Betty, two eggs. You wouldn't want me not to keep my strength up, would you?'

The woman laughed. 'There are a lot of rude things I might say in answer to that,' she replied.

'I can imagine.'

Sex between these two was an uninhibited affair which each of them enjoyed with more than usual keenness.

At the table Berry lit a cigarette and asked, 'How's the coffee coming along?'

'Ready in a moment. Give me a chance. You want everything all at once.'

'Sorry, old girl, sorry.'

He studied her through the little cloud of cigarette smoke which for a moment hung over the table. Wearing the gear which suited her best, an open-necked shirt and slacks. Tall and thin. Too thin, really. You couldn't call her a beauty, but good-looking in a hard way. Well, that suited him, he liked 'em hard....

She brought over two large cups of steaming coffee and sat opposite him.

'The bacon will be a couple of minutes yet,' she said. 'Give me a cigarette.'

He tossed a packet across and leant towards her with his lighter. A long deep inhalation, a plume of smoke blown out and the almost ecstatic pleasure of the true addict....

'God, marvellous the first of the day, almost the best, too, isn't it? I don't know how people cope who don't smoke.'

'Big Boy doesn't smoke.'

The woman shook her head in a little gesture of distaste, 'Big Boy doesn't smoke, joke or poke as far as I can see. I suppose he gets his fun out of life but,' she shook her head again, 'not my type.'

The man raised his cup.

'Der Tag.'

She lifted hers in reply.

'Der Tag, indeed. Here's luck to us.'

'Nervous?'

She laughed. 'Yes. Yes, I am. It would be silly to say that I am not. I wouldn't say *frightened* exactly; but nervous, yes. Butterflies in the tummy. The sort of feeling I always get when I'm up on a fresh horse and there's jumping to do. Incidentally it's the local point-to-point today so there'll probably be more traffic on the roads than usual.'

'What time does it start?'

'I suppose the first race will be one o'clock.'

'And the last?'

'Four-thirty probably. Not earlier anyway.'

'That's all right then. You'll be home and dry before they
start coming away. It's rather a good thing really, the more
horse boxes knocking about the better. What about that
bacon?'

The woman brought the plate of eggs and bacon from the
stove and set it in front of him.

'You're not having anything?' he asked.

She shook her head. 'Afraid of putting on weight.'

'You women make a fetish of this weight thing. You're
too damned thin as it is.'

'And you men are never satisfied. When we are thin you
leave us to go and smother yourself in the curves of some
overweight barmaid; and if we put on a bit of weight ourselves you want to know what's happened to our figures.'

He grinned. 'Unsatisfactory creatures, aren't we?'

'Very—except at times. Switch on the radio, it's half past.'

A small transistor set stood on the table; Berry leant
across and switched it on.

'...the whole of the south-west area should have a fine dry
day with plenty of sunshine and temperatures slightly above
average for the time of year....'

He switched off again and said, 'Sounds as though it's
going to be O.K. That was the one thing that might foul it
up, if they had fog on Dartmoor.'

'But suppose something else goes wrong, suppose it *does*
get fouled up somehow?'

'That will be up to Big Boy, won't it? It won't be any skin
off our nose. And you can say what you like about Big Boy
but he plays fair. He gives you a job to do and he tells you
how to do it. As long as you do it the way he says you get
paid.'

'So we shall get our five thousand?'

'That's absolutely certain. That's the way Big Boy has got
where he is. He says something and it happens. Someone
gets in his way, Big Boy says rub him out and, by Christ, the
fool gets rubbed out. He says he wants a job done and he'll

pay you five thousand for doing it and if you do the job the money's there.'

'Five thousand isn't all that much today.'

Berry laughed. 'Now who isn't satisfied? We are having all expenses paid and picking up five thousand quid on top of them. It may be nothing to some people; but, believe me, money like that doesn't grow on trees, even today.'

'What are we going to do when this little lot is over? Go back to the One-O-One?'

'Possibly. But I've a feeling that the One-O-One is worked out as far as we are concerned. Lately the Law has been shewing a bit more interest in the place. Time to move on probably.'

'Where to?'

'We might take a pub in the country somewhere.'

'Law-abiding, hard-working citizens?'

'We might give it a try.'

'Never. You're not the type. And I'm not either. We neither of us want to put down roots.'

When breakfast was finished the man lit his own first cigarette of the day and glanced at the clock.

'About four and a half hours to the off,' he said. 'This will be the worst part of it, doing nothing all morning. Let's go and look at the hidey-hole.'

Together they went out by the kitchen door and crossed the small yard at the back of the house.

As with all houses built on the moor when this one had been (it was some fifty or sixty years old) the accommodation for horses had been almost as important as accommodation for humans. The stabling at Castlecroft had originally been designed for three horses—stalls for two and a loose box. Nowadays only the loose box served its original purpose and as the two of them entered the stable Berry's grey gelding turned to greet them.

The space that had once been two stalls was littered with odds and ends of garden equipment, a good deal of it useless, left behind by the former tenants.

The woman put her hand through the bars of the loose-box door and gave the grey a friendly pat.

'You ought to be riding him to the point-to-point,' Berry said.

'Me in a point-to-point? I'd be scared stiff.'

'Not you. Never. You wouldn't be scared of anything.'

At the end of the stable a wall ladder ran vertically up into the loft above; the man and woman went up it and stood for a moment in the dark loft whilst their eyes grew accustomed to the diminishing light.

About half the loft was taken up by bales of hay, in the other half was scattered the sort of indiscriminate collection of odds and ends which any household accumulates and discards in the course of years—an old travelling-trunk with a domed lid, the wheel of a bicycle, two billiard cues. On the end wall of the loft a length of baler twine and some sacking hung from nails.

What was not easily detectable by the eye was that the length of the loft did not correspond exactly to the length of the stable below it. Anyone who went to the trouble of getting a tape measure to work would have been intrigued to find that the loft was three feet shorter than the stable underneath.

Big Boy's instructions had been 'Get yourself established there. Accepted. And then make a safe hiding-place. An old place like that with outbuildings, it ought not to be too difficult....'

Berry was a useful person with his hands and enjoyed D.I.Y. projects and after a careful survey of all the possibilities came to the conclusion that the best bet would be to build a false wall at the end of the loft shutting off a narrow space beyond it.

He now took the sacking off its nails and lifted a panel from the middle of the plywood wall which he had put up.

The space beyond was narrow—only three feet—but it ran the full width of the loft; three bricks had been knocked out of the end wall to let in air and at least some light and a chair and a mattress had been installed.

Berry surveyed it with sardonic amusement. 'The poor sod will think he's back in Dartmoor,' he said. 'Personally I doubt if we'll need it really. Provided the getaway plan works, why should anyone come looking for him here, fifty miles away? But Big Boy's orders are put him in the hidey-hole so in the hidey-hole he's got to go.'

'Still, they might come looking.'

'That's why he's going to be up here, just in case.'

'And what about the motor-bike?'

'Straight into the pond at the end of the garden. Long after we've gone somebody will find it and wonder how the hell it got there; but we shan't be worrying about it then.'

The woman nodded. 'And everything was all right last night?' she asked.

It was not the first time she had asked the same question, but if the man felt any annoyance at the repetition he took pains to hide it; he understood her feeling of nervousness; in the circumstances he thought a little nervousness was excusable; indeed, he felt a little nervous himself.

'Not to worry,' he told her. 'Everything went like clockwork. Twenty pounds of gellymix is hidden amongst the sacking on the floor of that hut waiting for Lenny Dawson to tell it when to go off.'

Again the woman nodded.

'I wonder what he's feeling like now,' she said. . . .

At that moment Lenny Dawson was feeling considerably shaken. Coming back from the exercise yard into the main hall and then up the iron staircase to the first landing the prisoner immediately in front of him had slipped and twisted his ankle. Normally any happening of this sort, any incident out of the usual routine, was a welcome diversion; when every day is a long dull uniformity of predictable greyness the slightest pinpoint of unexpected light is something to be made the most of.

''E's twisted it,' somebody said. 'Look at the size of it already.'

The man sitting on the ground looked with satisfaction at an already discernible swelling. This meant hospital for a day or two, surely; hospital was something slightly different and even the slightest variation of monotony was precious.

But Lenny was scared stiff for a moment or two.

Christ, that might have been me, he kept telling himself, and then where should I have been? Me laid up with a twisted ankle and everything fixed and ready outside—that is, if everything really *is* fixed and ready outside.

He thought it would be; a man couldn't help wondering and worrying a bit; but he thought everything would be O.K. With Big Boy it always was; but then, of course, against that comforting thought he couldn't help remembering that the bank job in Croydon High Street had been laid on by Big Boy and *that* had gone wrong.... 'By God, it went wrong,' he reflected, 'or I wouldn't be in this bloody awful place.'...You couldn't foresee everything, legislate for every possible contingency...nobody could, not even Big Boy.... No good worrying, though; he knew what the plan was down to the last detail; and it was a good plan, trust Big Boy for that....

But suppose, suppose...suppose it had been me who slipped on the iron stairway and twisted an ankle; but it wasn't, he kept reminding himself, it *wasn't*; no good supposing. All the same he wasn't happy about the gellymix fuse. 'There'll be five and eight marked on it,' he had been told. 'That means minutes; just turn it to which you think best according to what's happened, where people are and so forth.' It had all sounded simple enough, but the trouble was he had no idea what the fuse would look like, what size it would be, whether the '5' and '8' markings would be clear enough to be seen easily and quickly in the dark interior of the hut ... and then the motor-cycle; he could ride one, of course; at one time he had been one of a tearaway gang on motor-cycles, all noise and speed and hell generally; but that had been a few years ago; still, he supposed it would all come back to him, 'that is, if the bloody thing starts,' he thought.... Supposing it doesn't start; supposing 'they' change their minds and there isn't a working party at all to-day; or 'they' take us somewhere else, not to Farthinghoe at all....

In the middle of the morning one of the prison officers spoke to him and said, 'Outside working party for you this afternoon, Lenny. O.K.?'

Lenny nodded. He desperately wanted to ask, 'Is it Farthinghoe again?' but he thought it best not to; best not to shew any interest or excitement; best not to shew anything; so he just nodded.

Now he found that the palms of his hands were sweating a little.... The thing had started now; this was it; it was all going to work out as Big Boy had arranged. Or was it? Was something going to crop up that nobody could foresee? ...

Surprised that Lenny didn't answer, the prison officer was looking at him a little curiously.

'You all right, Lenny?' he asked. 'I can get you off if you don't want to go.'

'No. I'll go. I'm O.K. I'll go.'

As soon as he had uttered the words he was quite certain that he had said them too eagerly.... Why the hell should he be as keen as all that to go? The screw would suspect something.... Christ, what a start....

But the screw seemed satisfied and went away.

Lenny shut his eyes and forced himself to go over in his mind for the hundredth time, but now very slowly and deliberately, all that had to happen, all the things that he had to do....

At one-thirty the outside working party assembled. There were ten men in it and there were eight warders to look after them, four unarmed, four carrying carbines.

The unlocking of doors to go through; the counting as they went through; the locking up again after they had gone through—the routine was such an ingrained part of the men's lives now that most of them hardly noticed it.

But Lenny noticed it. When the last door was locked behind him and he heard the metallic *click* of the warden's key he thought *That's the last time I shall hear that sound, if I'm lucky,* and suddenly he was shaken by fear, the whole enterprise seemed monstrously impossible...gellymix—he wasn't a gellymix man; and the motor-cycle—he hadn't ridden a motor-cycle in years. *Christ, I shall need some luck,* he thought, *I shall need all the luck that's going....*

The ten prisoners were counted into the waiting coach and four warders got in after them; the four armed warders got into a car behind.

The driver of the bus had a two-way walkie-talkie set in his cab and he was protected behind and on both sides by a network of steel wire.

'All happy?' the chief warder asked.

'We'll be laughing ourselves to death in a minute,' the wag of the party answered. 'You'll 'ave us rolling in the aisles with it.'

But in a sense they *were* happy; for a few hours at least they were outside the walls. The moor wasn't much to look at; it was their enemy and every man inside knew that; but at least looking at it gave some illusion of temporary freedom.

'Next stop Farthinghoe Quarry. All fares, please.'

The traditional joke earned the traditional laugh and the chief warder was pleased to hear it. 'Get 'em laughing a bit and you steer clear of trouble' was his motto. Not that he expected any trouble. He was an experienced man. He was used to the outside-working-party routine. He knew it all backwards. It would all happen as it ought to happen. According to the rules and regulations. Count; split up; march. The tried and known routine. Nothing unusual, nothing out of the ordinary....

Lenny was sitting halfway up the mini-coach on the right-hand side; he knew the man next to him and they had spoken occasionally. They sat in silence for a while now until Lenny's companion said, 'Nice sunny day. Proper point-to-point weather.'

Lenny had only a vague idea of what a point-to-point was. Something to do with racing he knew; but exactly what? He didn't want to talk; he had too much to think about; and yet, in a way, he *did* want to talk; there was too much to think about; just for the moment he was scared, dead scared and that was the truth of it. All of a sudden he desperately wanted to empty his bladder.

He thought it best to answer something.

'You a racing man?' he asked.

The man next to him gave a short, despairing laugh. 'God, I'd give something to be on a horse again,' he said. 'God Almighty, would I not! ...'

Lenny allowed himself to smile.... Thank god, Big Boy didn't dream up a horse, he thought; no bloody horse for me. I don't want to be on any horse. A twin-cylinder Norton will do me—*if it's there*...but it would be there; Big Boy would fix it...a clump of bushes on the fringe of the quarry, he had been told; there'll be something white stuck in it, a piece of paper or a bit of rag, just as though it had blown there....

'Farthinghoe. All change.'

They laughed at that as well. Why not? Laughs were scarce enough and the poorest excuse for one was welcome.

The warders got out first and the chief warder stood by the bus exit.

'Let's have you,' he said and automatically counted them as they came out.

Meanwhile the four armed warders had got out of their car and had begun to station themselves on the perimeter of the scene and the second warder had gone to the store-hut and was unlocking it.

Lenny watched him fascinated. He didn't like the second warder. *The bugger will look in and see the bomb and the whole thing will be finished before it's started,* he thought....

But all the warder did was to unlock the padlock and pull the door of the hut open and stand by it to make sure that only one prisoner went in at a time.

'Right,' the chief warder said, 'that'll be six picks, then, and four shovels. One at a time, you know the drill.'

The men went in one by one, took a pick or shovel from the store ranged against one wall of the hut and came out again.

'Right. You stand over there. Next one....'

By bending down and pretending to be doing up his shoe lace Lenny managed to be the last man in.

Inside the hut it was dark and the difficulty of seeing was increased by the fact that the only light coming in was largely blocked by the body of the man entering the doorway.

'Shovel for you, Lenny,' he was told.

'O.K.'

His mouth was dry and he had difficulty in answering. His answer came queerly and he was quite sure the screw would notice something. There were only two shovels remaining, leaning against the wall on his right. The centre of the floor was bare but there was an untidy heap of some sacking and an old bag or two at the far end.

Three steps took him to it. His heart was thumping and on a sudden he actually felt scared. He wasn't a gellymix man and he didn't trust the stuff...suppose the bloody thing

blows up when I touch it, he thought.... He moved one of
the sacks to one side, and fear turned to gratitude.... Good
old Big Boy, puts the fear of God into you if you don't play
ball with him but, by Christ, he doesn't let you down; he
says a thing, it happens....

It was nestling in the sacking, a sort of box, innocent
enough looking, with a dial on top like a small saucer.

The numbers '5' and '8' were plainly marked on it just as
he had been told they would be.

He realized that he hadn't taken enough notice of the
disposition of things outside to decide whether five minutes
or eight would be the best interval to allow for.

'Come on, man,' the screw called.

Lenny bent down and turned the pointer on the dial to a
spot halfway between the '5' and the '8'.

He backed out of the hut carrying his shovel.

'I thought you had taken root in there.'

'I was picking a good one.'

'Well, let's see you do some good work with the bloody
thing. Right; with that other gang, over there.'

The warder shut the door of the hut and locked it. There
was not the slightest need to lock it, the action was purely
mechanical.

The chief warder called out, 'All right, then. Get yourselves sorted out. Two gangs of five. Three picks and two
shovels in a gang. One lot where we finished off last time,
close to here; the others away over there to the left.'

By good luck Lenny was in the gang sent to start work
some little distance away.

There were five men in the gang and two warders in
charge of them. Whilst the senior of the two warders was
saying something Lenny's eyes were sweeping the edge of the
quarry.

... Good old Big Boy again, the rugged clump of bushes
were there on the rim of the quarry and, just as though it
had been blown there by a chance wind (and not carefully

put in place by Baillie-Wilson at two o'clock that morning), a piece of white rag fluttered.

... It looked a hell of a long way off to Lenny, all of a hundred yards.... The four armed warders were taking up their stations on the perimeter of a circle some distance away from the centre of things.... If a man ran for it the whistles would blow and he might get a bullet in the leg or in the back—unless, of course, there was such a hell of a noise and confusion that for ten or fifteen vital seconds nobody quite knew what was happening.

... The great thing was to get as close to the quarry edge as possible to cut down that hundred yards....

'What are you in such a hurry about, Lenny?'

'I want to get started.'

'Got plenty of time ahead of you, haven't you? What do you want to do—shift the whole bloody moor by yourself?'

Laughter. Lenny joined in. One of the golden rules of the place: always laugh at the bastards' jokes.... In God's name, he thought, how long is seven minutes.... He was suddenly afraid that he had been a fool: 'Put it at 5 or 8,' he had been told, and like the idiot he was he had put it between the two; very likely the thing didn't work if the pointer was be—

Then it happened.

Lenny had been expecting it; but he hadn't been expecting *this*. He was totally unprepared for the enormity of noise which twenty pounds of gellymix made when it exploded.

The whole quarry was filled not only with noise but with blast and reverberation.

Lenny had no idea it would be like this. *'Jesus God all-bloody-mighty,'* he exclaimed and just as he had been told to do he started to run....

He was more than two-thirds of the way towards the clump of ragged bushes before the noise and the reverberations of it died away.

The armed warder who should have done something about the escaping prisoner was quite unaware of what was happening. He was staring in horrified fascination at the spot where the hut had been. He had been idly watching the driver of the mini-bus who had got out of his cab and seated himself on the ground in a patch of sunshine leaning against the hut, pulling a newspaper out of his pocket to have a quiet read.

'Lucky blighter,' the warder had been thinking. 'Some people have got the cushy jobs all right.'

Then it happened.

Now there was no hut; and no driver sitting propped up comfortably against it; there was still reverberating noise and a great cloud of dust and smoke and pieces of timber and bits of metal and bit of God alone knew what else raining down all over the place....

Lenny ran as he had never run before in his life, forcing his out-of-condition legs to do what he didn't know they were capable of doing. He thought his pumping heart would burst; but he was at the edge of the quarry and scrambling over into the ragged bushes before the first whistle blew....

'As soon as they get over the shock of the stuff going off the bastards will start blowing their effing whistles,' Lenny had been told.

Now it was happening.

But it was too late. And, ironically, it was at least for a vital moment or two counterproductive.

Only one warder had spotted the running man and when he blew his whistle everybody automatically looked towards him to see what he was blowing for; by the time he had shouted and gesticulated Lenny was out of the quarry and in among the bushes.

It was there. The lovely, superb, marvellous, incredible motor-cycle. Upright, the rear wheel jacked up on its stand.

There was more whistle-blowing now and some shouting.

Lenny pulled the Norton off its stand and threw his leg over it. He twisted the handle-bar control and gave the self-starter a hell of a kick.

Without a suggestion of hesitation or reluctance the engine roared into splendid life.

Lenny engaged first gear, let in the clutch and shot away along the rough moorland track. Behind him the whistles and the shouting died to a diminuendo.

Indescribable waves of relief and satisfaction and savage animal enjoyment surged through him.

'Christ Almighty,' he shouted against the roar of his engine. 'I've made it. I'm away.'

'If you can get away, if all the hut business works,' Lenny had been told, 'you'll be able to get through Ashburton and as far as Buckfastleigh before they can get anything organized about road blocks and so on. That's certain. And just outside Buckfastleigh, the A384, you know what to look out for.'

Lenny knew what to look for but he had to get to Buckfastleigh first. The going was rough over the moorland track, and at the speed he was making he had a job to keep the Norton upright. Lucky for him it was dry and so there was no danger of getting bogged.

After a couple of hundred yards he broke out onto the metalled road and swung right-handed for Ashburton.

Now he could really let the engine work for him; there was no traffic about and his only danger was the chance of meeting a speed cop.... No speed cops, he was in luck....

'A384.' He saw it marked up on a signpost as he flashed by and seeing it made him feel good; it seemed friendly somehow.

Suddenly a little spate of traffic on the road (all coming towards him; he was going too fast to be overtaken by anything) and then Ashburton already.

He forced himself to slow up going through Ashburton though he hated doing so; speed was equated with escape in his mind and cutting it down felt almost like giving himself up.

Turn right at Ashburton and then it was a different matter. Now he was on the A38, the main Exeter-to-Plymouth road and there was all too much traffic about.

He made the best time he could praying for the A384 to shew up again on the left. It came at last and he swung off the big main road with relief. This was the Buckfastleigh turn, and a mile and a half along it lay his goal.

'You'll have to keep your eyes skinned or you'll miss it,' he had been warned. So he kept his eyes skinned and once again, grudgingly, abated his pace.

Even so he very nearly missed it. The turning was on him before he realized it, the merest suggestion of an old green lane leading off to the left, the entrance to it half-obscured by overgrown bushes.

He cut the engine off, braked desperately hard and wrenching the Norton round just in time to avoid the stump of an old tree ended up in a heap at the green-lane entrance.

For a few seconds he was half-knocked out, then his senses cleared and he was aware of a woman saying, 'Are you all right? I've got the horse box here, come on'....

Betty had got the horse box in position at exactly ten minutes past two. She wanted to give herself time to get well established and everything set and yet not to have to wait for too long for fear anyone noticed her and became curious.

She ran the horse box off the road and for some twenty yards along the green lane until it was hidden from view. Then she switched off the engine and let the tailboard down.

The horse inside moved his ears backwards and forwards and shifted a little on his feet expecting to be led out.

'Steady, Rufus,' she soothed him. 'This isn't your outing, old boy.'

She lit a cigarette and glanced at her wristwatch. Two-fifteen, so there ought not to be much more than a quarter of an hour to wait. She walked along the green lane to make sure that there wasn't some unexpected obstruction in it. The lane was crescent-shaped and joined the road again after a few hundred yards. She walked the length of it and there were no snags, no obstructions, nothing to worry about.

She came back to the horse box and sat, smoking, on the lowered tailboard. She could hear traffic going by occasionally on the A384 but she couldn't see it, nor be seen by it. The horse moved impatiently and she spoke to it again. She threw away the butt of her cigarette and watched it burn safely away in the tangled grass at her feet.

... Two-thirty, her watch said, so now he ought to be coming. She got up and made sure that the tailboard was secure and the jacket, dungarees and cap ready.

It was whilst she was doing this that she heard the noise as the Norton slewed round to the left, lost balance and crashed to the ground.

The woman ran to the entrance of the green lane and there the machine was in a heap on the gravelly grass, the wheel spinning round and the man more or less underneath it....

He wasn't killed anyway, because she could see his head moving as she ran up to him.

'Are you all right?' she asked.

There was blood on his face but not a great deal of it. He answered something which she supposed was an affirmative so she went on, 'I've got the horse box here, so come on. Can you manage?'

Lenny was already managing. He felt shaken and he thought his leg was hurting, but couldn't be bothered to find out. He was already pulling at the heavy machine to get it upright again.

The woman helped him and said urgently, 'Come on, this way.'

'Is it far?' he asked.

'No, no, of course not. Just round the bend—here.'

There it was, indeed; waiting for him, once again just as Big Boy had planned.

The tailboard was down and the box divided down the middle by a partition. The left-hand side of it was occupied by a horse; the right-hand size was empty except for a stable rug and a bundle of clothes.

'In there?' he asked.

She nodded and warned him, 'Mind the tailboard; it's a bit slippery.'

His leg hurt like hell and he was pushing the Norton up into the box but he couldn't pay attention to it yet.

The horse shifted uneasily and whinnied a little at the unexpected fuss and commotion alongside. The woman said something reassuring to it and then to Lenny.

'Go on. You get in now and I'll shut the back up. You'll find some clothes on the floor. Better put the rug over the motor-bike.'

Lenny scrambled up beside the Norton and the box suddenly lost a lot of light as the back was pushed into position and bolted on the outside.

In less than thirty seconds he heard the comforting sound of the engine starting and then the horse box suddenly lurched forward and he was all but thrown off balance.

After about a minute the going was suddenly much smoother and he realized that they must be on the A384 again and heading for—he didn't know where they were heading for now; and he didn't care so long as it was away from Dartmoor. Big Boy's plan had worked like a dream so far and Lenny was content now to make himself comfortable in the cramped space alongside the motor-cycle and gingerly stretched out his painful leg. Presently a panel slid back behind the driving-seat and over her shoulder Betty called, 'You all right?'

'Yes. Fine.'

'Not cut or anything? I saw some blood.'

'Only a few scrapes. My leg hurts a bit.'

'Have you got those clothes on?'

'Just doing it now.'

It took him some little time to pull on the dungaree trousers, partly because the horse box swayed considerably, partly because of the injury to his leg.

When finally he had managed to get them on and the jacket as well he felt that another large step towards freedom had been taken.

The communicating panel slid open again.

'O.K.?'

'Yes. Fine.'

'Have you got the horse rug over the bike?'

'Yes, I've fixed that. Are we likely to be stopped?'

'I shouldn't think so. You got away all right, didn't you? I mean nobody actually on your heels, was there?'

'No fear,' Lenny laughed. 'I should think they are still getting over the bang. Christ, what a noise! I was scared stiff.'

'If we *are* stopped, you're James Baker and you work for me, help in the stables and so on, at Castlecroft. Get it?'

'James Baker. Castlecroft. Yes, O.K. What's your name?'

'You work for Captain and Mrs Berry. My name's Betty.'

'How long before we get there?'

'Depends on the traffic. I want to make it by four-thirty; might do a bit better. There's a point-to-point near home but we ought to be back before they all start coming away from that.'

After some moments he tapped on the panel and Betty slid it open.

'Have you got a fag on you?' he asked.

'Sorry,' Betty said, 'but not in the horse box; not with all the straw and the horse in it, and everything.'

'O.K., O.K.' He desperately wanted a smoke, but he could wait; he could wait; he was away, off the moor already and under Big Boy's protection; he could wait for his smoke....

He settled down and tried to get his leg comfortable.

Occasionally the woman slid back the panel to give him news of where they were.

'Just on the outskirts of Exeter, but the traffic doesn't seem to be too bad yet.'

'This bloody animal of yours is getting restive,' Lenny grumbled. 'Is he all right?'

'He's tired of being shut up.'

Lenny laughed explosively. 'Poor bugger,' he said. 'So am I.'

After Exeter Betty told him, 'Crediton next and a long run up the A377.'

'Where is this Castlecroft place?'

'On Exmoor, out in the wilds.'

'God, another bloody moor! Can't you speed up a bit? This leg of mine is beginning to hurt.'

'You can't take a horse box fast. We'll get your leg fixed as soon as we get back.'

After what seemed a long time to Lenny the woman spoke again.

'South Molton, so cheer up; this really is home territory now.'

'Thank God for that.'

With South Molton behind them it was very soon North Molton and then once again the real moorland road with no traffic about and home coming closer every minute.

When the entrance to Castlecroft shewed up ahead Betty glanced at her watch—4.25.

'Back in nice time for tea,' Berry had said, and that was just how it was turning out; everything had gone well.

Berry had been waiting anxiously for the last half-hour. He agreed that Big Boy's plan was a good one, probably the best one yet devised for getting a man out of Dartmoor. But things could go wrong. The gellymix bomb might be discovered by somebody before it was due to go off; the timing fuse might not work properly; and even if all that side of it went smoothly there was always the possibility of an accident to the horse box on the way back.

He had filled in his waiting-time inspecting—for the tenth time—the hiding-place in the loft and once more debating with himself the best way to get rid of the motor-cycle. In the end he returned to his original plan of running it into the deep pool at the end of the Castlecroft garden. 'Only,' he reminded himself, 'we must remember to obliterate any tyre marks.'

When he finally heard the horse box turning at the gate he glanced at his watch—well on time, even a minute or two before. It looked as though everything had gone all right, then.

He hurried forward and the woman jumped out of the driving-seat.

'Everything O.K.?' he asked.

She nodded, smiling.

'You weren't stopped?'

'No, nothing. Absolutely clear run. But,' she nodded towards the box, 'he's hurt his leg a bit.'

'Badly?'

'I don't think badly, no. He turned into the green lane where I was waiting too quickly and had a skid.'

'Let's get him out and the bike into the pond.'

Together they undid the fastenings of the back of the horse box and lowered it to the ground to form a ramp.

Lenny was sitting inside, close to the Norton from which the covering rug had fallen away.

The two men looked at one another.

'You're Lenny, eh?'

'That's it.'

'Glad to be out?'

'Christ, you can say that again.'

'Everything all right? The gellymix business and all that?'

'Went like a dream. God knows what it didn't throw up; just about everything I should think.'

'How's your leg?'

'It seems to be getting worse. I suppose I might have broken something; begins to feel like it.'

'Otherwise you're O.K.?'

'I feel a bit swimmy.'

'We'll soon have you lying down comfortably with a nice cup of tea. Come on, Betty, let's get the bike out first and then Lenny can see how bad his leg is.'

Together he and the woman manhandled the Norton down the ramp of the tailboard and pulled it back onto its stand on the gravel drive.

Then they turned to help Lenny out and as they were reaching up to give him a hand Betty said quietly and urgently, *'Don't look up; there's somebody watching us.'*

NINE

RACHEL WAS STRONGLY IN FAVOUR of Hooky's suggestion
that he might take a day off and go to the Exdale point-to-
point. She was a kindly and good person, but she had her
share of that vicarious interest which every woman feels in
the possibility of somebody else's romances.

When Hooky told her that at the Huntsman he had accidentally met a girl he knew in London and that she had invited him to join her party at the races Rachel was vastly
intrigued.

'Do you suppose she is somebody *special*?' she asked
Francis, talking the matter over with him later.

'All girls are special with Hooky; hadn't you noticed?'

'Oh, Francis, don't be horrible. Hooky's *nice.*'

'In some ways he's one of the nicest fellows I've ever met;
but Hooky as a husband....' Francis pulled a humorously
dubious face.

'I think you are being perfectly beastly.'

'Quite right, dear. Most men are.'

'Hooky will make some girl wonderfully happy.'

'I'm sure he has already made lots of girls wonderfully
happy—for a time.'

Rachel laughed. 'You old stick in the mud, you,' she said.
'But anyway there's no reason why he shouldn't go, is
there?'

'None at all. We shall both be here. The boy can be with
me in the yard, or with you in the house. As a matter of fact,
I think it would be a very good thing if the two of them had
a day's rest from one another.'

Hooky's conscience, which always had a struggle to keep its head above water, impelled him to give Simon the chance of going to the point-to-point as well. To his infinite relief the boy was as irritatingly superior about the subject as he was about nearly everything else.

'A point-to-point? I'm not absolutely clear what that is. Some form of horse-racing, I suppose?'

'Got it in one, chum. Some form of horse-racing. Three and a half miles of fair hunting country, if I remember the wording correctly, and the only time I was lunatic enough to take part in one I was scared out of my wits.'

'As I'm not even allowed to ride Cinders here in the farm I don't see why I should be expected to interest myself in watching other people racing.'

Hooky shut his eyes for a moment, but he kept his temper. 'You are not allowed to ride Cinders, boy-o, because that's the fiat. The word has gone forth. She-who-must-be-obeyed has said no and we harken and do as we are told.'

'That's the trouble with your generation—too much blind obedience.'

'If I even started to tell you the troubles with your generation, those scientific little ears of yours would get severely shocked.'

'I suppose you will be going to this racing business with a party of some kind?'

'You might put it that way.'

'No doubt you will all drink a lot.'

'I sincerely hope so.'

'And probably bet money on the outcome of each race?'

Hooky took a deep breath. Why Loeson senior should have gone to considerable trouble and expense to protect his singularly unattractive progeny from possible danger was becoming more and more difficult to understand.

'I expect I shall have my usual modest flutter,' he admitted.

'I'm afraid that doesn't appeal to me in the slightest,' Simon said dismissingly. 'I like making money, not losing it. I suppose you realize that a book is so made that the only person certain to win is the bookmaker? I can explain the mathematics of it to you if you like.'

'Some other time,' Hooky said with decision, 'some other time.'

When Hooky eventually drove away from Sheepsgate a great feeling of relief flooded over him. He was having a day off. And by God I've earned it, he thought. The boys in El Vino will never believe what I have subjected myself to down here.'

With Sheepsgate behind him and a wide and lively prospect of the moor opening out all round, his spirits rose rapidly. It was a perfect March day, clear and sharp and sunny. Overhead great white galleons of cloud sailed majestically across the blue oceans of the sky; it was spring in England, and an Englishman who possessed many of his country's virtues (and quite a few of its failings) was setting out to enjoy it in his venerable and beloved Jag.

The Exdale point-to-point was not one of the fashionable meetings; it was a smaller, more homely affair than many, but even so traffic began to thicken as Hooky got close to the spot where it was being held and when he finally arrived the slope of the hill which formed a natural grandstand was already thick with cars; the March sun shone on them and glinted off their shining metalwork.

'You can hardly miss the Fenton Park barouche,' Fenella had told him. 'It's the size of a small battleship and will be close up to the finishing-post as Tony is one of the judges.'

Hooky found a berth for the Jag and went exploring on foot. Fenella, he was delighted to discover, had been absolutely right. The Fenton Park Rolls, a venerable and magnificent specimen that made no concessions whatsoever to meagre present-day standards, was easily spotted.

Such a huge party was based on it that Hooky made no attempt to sort out who they all were. For the most part they were young and colourful and gay; the most colourful and the gayest of them all, Hooky thought, was Fenella. Fenella was dressed very much *pour le sport*; Hooky was quite certain he had never seen white riding-breeches and hacking-jacket worn more bewitchingly. As he came up to the party she was standing, glass in hand, at the rear of the Rolls by a picnic table carrying a splendidly reassuring assortment of bottles.

'You've made it,' she cried. 'Oh, Hooky, I'm so glad.'

'Don't tell me you're actually taking part in this dangerous business?' he asked.

'The Ladies' Race. Angela's letting me ride Gaiety Girl for her. I'm simply terrified.'

Hooky was introduced to his host and hostess, and a footman in a striped waistcoat who was presiding at the drinks table asked him solicitously what he would care to have. 'Buck's fizz, sir, or Pimms, or of course anything else you may fancy.' It was already clear to Hooky that his day off was going to prove a success.

'And how are you getting on?' Fenella asked him.

Hooky held up his just-acquired glass. 'At the moment, splendidly.'

'Ah, but I mean the job. Still holding it down to everyone's satisfaction?'

'If I get discharged, it will be for mayhem,' Hooky assured her. 'Scientific and Sarcastic Youth strangled by Tormented Tutor is the sort of headline the El Vino boys will come up with. I shall expect you to visit me in jail.'

'I think the whole idea of putting people in prison is barbaric.'

'Believe you me, quite a few of the people who get sent there are fairly barbarous too!'

'Life's a pretty wretched affair sometimes, Hooky.'

'Life's intolerable—if you think about it. I'm a great believer in non-thought as the sovereign remedy for most of our ills.' He handed back his already-emptied glass to Striped Waistcoat. 'Another go of non-thought, if I may, please,' he said.

The slim girl in riding-kit watched him with amusement. 'How's the autobiography coming along?' she asked.

'The bright morning of action tends to lose its radiance in the dark labyrinth of composition—my favourite quote from good old Chu Ling; and, by Heaven, the old Chink was right. As I lived it, it was all good fun; but it's dull stuff when I try to churn it out on paper.'

'You're not a writing animal, Hooky.'

'You can say that again. Believe me, meeting you down here and having this day out is just about preserving my sanity.'

'I shall go down in history as the woman who saved Hooky Hefferman's sanity.'

'You'll go down in history as the woman who did Hooky Hefferman's finances a lot of good if you can tell me what's going to win the first race.'

'There's a great buzz for Oh Kay.'

'Is your money following the buzz?'

The attractive little face made a moue of amused indifference. 'I keep my money in my pocket.'

'Wise woman,' Hooky said; but he himself, of course, had no intention of being wise. *The trouble with you Hooky, or rather one of the troubles with you, is that when you get anywhere near a race-course or a gaming-table you lose all sense of proportion.* More than once Hooky's formidable old aunt had thundered the words at him, and he would have been the first to acknowledge their truth.

Wisdom was not for Hooky on a day out such as this; he was shortly confronting the florid face and extravagantly checkered suit of Honest Joe who instantly recognized him as a sporting gent and a sucker of the first water.

'Any one you like, sir, any one you like. Evens the favourite. Any one you like.'

Hooky consulted Honest Joe's board. Oh Kay was marked at even money. There was a horse at four to one, a couple at five to one, one at ten to one and the outsider of the party at sixteen to one. But the sixteen-to-one outsider was called Perfect Pest.

Like all gamblers Hooky was a great believer in signs and portents. 'If they don't mean anything,' he would frequently argue, 'what are they sent to us for?' Perfect Pest was good enough for him. . . .

He drew out his wallet. 'I'll have ten quid on Perfect Pest,' he said.

Honest Joe's face, heavily grooved with the lines of alcohol, sex, villainy and evasiveness, broke into a genial smile; it was pleasant to know that he had been right about the sucker. He handed the ticket over with a flourish. 'One hundred and sixty to ten Perfect Pest,' he said. 'A pleasure to take a bet from a sporting gent.'

The sporting gent went back to the vantage point of the Fenton Park Rolls to watch the race. Most of the gay young party there had backed the favourite. Nobody, Hooky gathered, thought anything of the outsider's chances.

The starter's white flag went up and the 'They're off' was shouted. It was easy enough to follow the progress of Perfect Pest since he was the only grey in the field. He instantly shot away at full gallop, took the first fence much too fast and almost came to grief over it, managed somehow to stay upright and continued on his headlong course.

Halfway round the first time the grey was out on his own, fifteen lengths ahead of everything else. A young wiseacre standing next to Hooky lowered his glasses. 'Fancy riding a race like that,' he said. 'The horse is just running away with him. Pathetic.'

When they went into the country for the second time Perfect Pest was still leading but only by three or four lengths. The favourite was still kept well at the back.

At the awkward fence when they turned the second horse jumped badly and came down bringing the third horse with it.

'Hell's bells,' the young wiseacre groaned. 'That's my fiver gone for a burton.'

Perfect Pest was still in front, but Oh Kay's jockey had now take stock of things and was already asking his mount to get going.

'That grey thing keeps batting along,' someone said.

'Yes, but look at the favourite. That's the way to ride a race. That chap knows what he's doing. He's had Oh Kay on the bit till a moment ago; now just look at him.'

Two fences from home the favourite and the outsider were together; Oh Kay made much the better jump and sailed happily into the lead.

'He's only got to stand up,' was the general verdict, 'and we are all home and dry.'

Fortunately for the bookmakers 'stand up' was the one thing the favourite failed to do; the horse had jumped impeccably up to date and he came to the last fence with a three-lengths lead and in no danger from anything. Over-confidence on the jockey's part? A mistake by a tiring horse? Possibly (extravagant thought) the gods intervening on behalf of suckers? Whatever the cause Oh Kay took the last fence in disastrous style, hitting the top of it hard and landing up in a heap on the floor. Perfect Pest's jump was by no means a good one but he got over and ran on to be an easy winner.

'Were you on it?' somebody asked.

'In a small way,' Hooky admitted.

'Lucky so-and-so.'

Hooky smiled.

'A pleasure to pay you, sir,' said Honest Joe; and he meant it; his commodious satchel was stuffed with money put trustingly on the favourite.

Between races Hooky and Fenella walked to the nearest fence to inspect it from close quarters. It looked alarmingly formidable to Hooky. 'Don't tell me you are going to jump over that damned great affair,' he said. 'It's as bad as the National.'

Fenella gave a nervous little laugh; her own race was only half an hour away and she was beginning to be acutely aware of the fact.

'It's rather shame-making to have to confess it,' she said, 'but this is when I start feeling scared. And I wouldn't say as much to many people, Hooky, I can assure you.'

'You can safely say it to me. I wouldn't go careering round this course for all the Teachers in Scotland. You're scared but you've got the guts to go and do it. That's something I like, Fenella.'

She gave a quick smile of gratitude. 'I'll remember that when I'm taking the first jump,' she said, 'but don't put any money on me, will you?'

'No fear. One of my firmest betting principles concerns the Ladies' Race at point-to-points: *back the ugly uns;* watch 'em going down to the post, and the rider whose face most closely resembles that of her mount—put your money on her. That's my motto, *back the ugly uns,* so obviously that rules you out.'

'A long-winded and roundabout compliment,' Fenella said with a sudden return to her prim manner, 'but, after all, any compliment is welcome—especially from a soldier of fortune.'

At the Fenton Park Rolls the money went unswervingly in one direction, on No. 7 Gaiety Girl: chestnut mare; aged; the property of Lady Angela Fenton; ridden by Miss F. D'Aubiac; white, blue star, blue and white hooped sleeves.

Honest Joe and his confrères rated Gaiety Girl's chances at twelve to one; but as the horses left the paddock on their long journey to the starting-post some rumour or whim of public fancy cut this price first down to nines and almost immediately to sevens.

'I suppose that means somebody must think she's got a chance,' Angela Fenton said.

'Do *you* think she has?' Hooky enquired.

His hostess laughed. 'Not much of a one really. But you never know. Things happen. Look at Oh Kay in the first race. Anyway, she'll give Fen a good ride. Fen will ride her beautifully. In case you haven't realized it, Mr Hefferman, that girl does everything she tackles well.'

Fenella did ride beautifully, cutting all her corners like a professional and cleverly correcting the one mistake Gaiety Girl made; but the pace was too hot and the other horses too good and at the finish the 'white, blue star, blue and white hooped sleeves' could do no better than come in a poor third.

'Well, she got placed, anyway,' Angela Fenton said.

'Thank heavens she got round in one piece,' was Hooky's comment. 'My heart was in my mouth every time she went over a fence.'

Angela glanced at him for a moment in amused interest.

The last race was at four-thirty, and as soon as that was over the Fenton Park crowd all flocked like homing pigeons to the rear of the hospitable Rolls and Striped Waistcoat started serving tea. A radio was switched on. 'Any news?' somebody asked.

'Something about a chap getting away from Dartmoor.'

'He won't get far; they never do from Dartmoor.'

'Who cares, anyway? Turn it off, for God's sake.'

Hooky congratulated Fenella on her riding. She made a slight grimace. 'Third isn't the same as first, is it? But, still, I did stay on and I suppose that's something.'

'You bet it's something,' Hooky assured her. 'For me it would approach the miraculous. How long are you going to be down here, Fen?'

'Oh, well—that depends on a number of things. But Angela's is always full of people coming and going, so an extra guest or two doesn't matter. I expect I shall stay on for a few days, anyway.'

'Do that thing,' Hooky said. 'I'd like you to. We'll be seeing one another.'

AT SHEEPSGATE, after Hooky's departure in the Jag, Rachel said, 'You were silly not to go to the point-to-point, Simon. It's always the greatest fun.'

'Horse-racing doesn't appeal to me—particularly as I'm not allowed to ride.'

Rachel held up a warning finger. 'Now, now, Simon. For Heaven's sake don't start all that again; we've had it out quite often enough already. There's lots to do, so make yourself busy.'

'*What* is there to do?'

'Well, for one thing Francis is fencing in Little Twitchell and you can give him a hand; he'd be glad of some help.'

Simon made his way without any marked show of enthusiasm to the small enclosure some distance from the house where Francis was repairing an ancient post-and-rail fence. In spite of his unenthusiastic start the boy became quite interested in the job and the two of them worked together throughout the morning. At lunch-time they were summoned indoors by the ringing of a large bell and Rachel's voice supplementing it, 'Come on, you two men. Wash and brush up. Everything's ready.'

'Everything', when they sat down to it, was strong, thick soup; a steak-and-kidney pudding; vegetables straight out of the garden; home-made bread and lashings of butter and a lovely piece of Lancashire cheese.

'When you marry, Simon,' Francis advised, 'be sure you pick a woman who's a good cook. It's important.'

'I expect I shall hire a cook, like my father does,' the boy answered.

Francis caught his wife's eye and for a fleeting second they both smiled slightly. . . .

When Francis was ready to set off for Little Twitchell again in the afternoon Simon said he didn't want to accompany him. 'I'm tired of fencing,' he said.

'Help me, then,' Rachel suggested.

'What doing?'

'I'm going to be making jam, and what I urgently want is all these old jars thoroughly washed out and dried. If you would do that for me it would be a great help.'

'Where shall I do it?'

'We shall get in one another's way here, so the best thing is for you to take the whole lot into the little pantry at the end of the passage whilst I'm getting on with things in the kitchen.'

'O.K. I don't mind having a go.'

When the boy went out of the kitchen Francis said, 'Not what you would call an enthusiastic helper, is he?'

'Oh, well, as long as he's kept busy doing something. . . .'

Simon got through his chore of washing out and drying the jam jars reasonably thoroughly and with expedition. Rachel was still heavily engaged in the kitchen and the boy left the little pantry and wandered out into the yard at the back of the house. When he walked past the stable Cinders was looking out over the half-door. Simon went in and spoke a word to the mare, who put her ears back a little. Saddle, bridle were hanging on the wall and Simon eyed them. Then he walked to the half-door and looked out. There wasn't a sign or sound of anybody.

He went back into the stable and the mare fidgeted a little on her feet; she wanted to be taken out, but she wasn't at all sure that she wanted to be taken out by a stranger. To

Simon a horse was merely something that moved, a means of locomotion, not as good as driving the Jag, of course, but better than plodding round on your feet and a bit of fun and excitement when there was nothing else to be had. He was no horseman and never would be one and he had no conception of Cinders as an individual with likes, dislikes and a temper of her own. The boy lifted the saddle off its rest and approached the mare; he had watched Rachel saddle and bridle up half a dozen times and, always confident in his own ability to do anything, he saw no reason why he shouldn't manage the business successfully.

The mare put her ears back and moved a little uneasily but submitted, and Simon got the saddle on and the girths done up without any trouble.

This early success pleased him. Nothing to it, he thought. He had rather more difficulty with the bridle, and it was more by good luck than anything else that he eventually got it on.

He looked out over the half-door of the stable. Everything was still quiet; there was no sign or sound of anybody. He turned back into the stable and lifted Rachel's riding-crop from off the hook where it hung; then opening the door he led the mare out into the yard.

Six yards brought them to the edge of the moor and there was still not a sound from the house (at that moment Rachel had her head inside the oven of her Aga cooker).

Immensely pleased and excited by the success so far of his adventure Simon now essayed the business of mounting. He made a sprawling hash of it and only the fact that the mare wanted to have somebody on her back and then to be away over the moor induced her to put up with his clumsiness.

Eventually Simon got himself into the saddle, found his stirrup irons and began to feel a bit settled. The mare instantly set off at a smart trot and within a couple of minutes horse and rider were hidden from the house by the dip in the ground.

Simon was exhilarated by his escapade; but he had only the most rudimentary idea of how to rise to a horse's trot and he was finding the jog-jog-jog motion uncomfortable; so, too, was the mare; it was now becoming clear to her that she had a very troublesome human being on her back and she was losing her temper; she allowed herself to be reined back into a walk and for some minutes both horse and rider went more easily.

They went on like this—bouts of awkward trotting interspersed with periods of walking—for some little time and Simon began to feel more at home. He was getting into the rhythm of rising to the trot, but it was when Cinders, growing tired of the walk-trot-walk business, broke into a hack canter that the boy really began to enjoy himself.

This was more like it, he thought, and to emphasize his sense of pleasure he brought the crop down with a good hard thwack on the mare's flank. Instantly Cinders shot forward at a gallop, furiously outraged. If Rachel ever did put a stranger up on the mare it was always with the warning, 'If you carry a crop, for Heaven's sake don't use it; she simply won't have it.'

Simon was alarmed at the sudden change of pace and was still more alarmed when the saddle suddenly began to shift under him. When saddling up he had fallen into the usual beginner's error of not tightening his girths properly and now he was paying the penalty. He began to shout at the mare to stop, and the shouts and the slipping saddle were too much for her; she bolted; and Simon, an unwilling passenger on an uncontrollable horse going at full tilt across the open moor, was very scared indeed.

Nothing he could do made any difference to the head-long gallop they were travelling at, and in fact he very soon gave up all attempts to do anything except stay on. The mare was going as fast as she could travel and after five minutes at full gallop she would have been happy to take a bit of a breather. For a couple of hundred yards she had been careering down a long slope at the bottom of which ran the remains of a very ancient trackway; Cinders didn't fancy galloping up the slope on the other side, so having hit the grassy trackway she jinked hard to the right with scarcely a break in her speed. An experienced polo-player would have had a job to stay in the saddle in the circumstances and Simon didn't stand a chance; he shot off unceremoniously and cracked his shoulder hard against a large stone half-hidden in the grassy edge of the track. Freed of her unsatisfactory rider and still worried by the badly adjusted saddle the mare cantered off into the distance.

The force with which he was thrown all but knocked Simon out and for a few minutes the boy lay winded and virtually unconscious. When he was able to pull himself together a little and to sit up and look round he began to feel alarmed. The horse had disappeared, his shoulder was hurting and he had no idea where he was.

He stood up, a little groggily at first, and rather aimlessly looked around. Whichever way he turned the moor looked exactly the same. He hadn't the vaguest notion which direction to go, and after a moment or two of indecision he decided to take the line of least resistance and to walk along the ancient trackway.

Before long the trackway—such as it was—petered out entirely and merged once more into the unbroken turf of the moor; but now the ground had risen slightly and on the horizon Simon could see a small clump of trees. What, or where, they were he had no idea, but in that otherwise unbroken landscape at least they were something, a mark he could guide himself by. He decided to walk as straight as he could towards them and to see what happened when he got there.

Having a definite goal to aim at made him feel a little better, but five minutes later his rising spirits were rudely shattered when the ground suddenly gave way under his

tread and he found himself almost up to his knees in oozing mud.

Bog! Francis and Rachel had warned both him and
Hooky about it.

'You've got to keep your eyes skinned for it,' Francis had
said. 'Of course, you might walk across the moor all day
long and never strike any, but there are patches here and
there and some of them can be very nasty.'

Bog was frightening; and the boy was thoroughly scared
now. For a horrible minute he wasn't sure that he was going
to be able to draw his feet out of the black oozing stuff he
had stumbled into, but in the end he managed to fight the
few steps backwards onto land that he knew was safe.

He stood there frightened and trying to recover his com-
posure. By studying the ground in front of him closely he
thought he could detect the boggy area. At any rate, there
was a patch which was considerably greener than the sur-
rounding grass and he concluded that this must be the dangerous part. The clump of trees on the crest was still his
object and he now made a wide cast to the right, keeping a
very close eye out for any suspiciously bright green patches
and treading very tentatively.

This sort of progress was slow work but eventually he arrived at the clump of three windswept trees without further
mishap, and having got there his spirits rose dramatically.
Beyond the slight ridge on which the trees stood the ground
sloped away to something the fifteen-year-old boy was beginning to feel he was never going to see again—a house and
buildings.

Simon looked at them with delight. His shoulder was
hurting badly, the bog episode had given him a thorough
scare and he was desperately in need of human company and
care. As he moved forward nearer the house a large motor-
vehicle was being driven towards it along the rough moorland road from the other side. There was a fence which the
boy negotiated with difficulty because of his shoulder;

twenty yards further on a privet hedge marked the boundary of the grounds; when Simon reached it he stood there for a moment or two watching. The motor-vehicle (he could see now that it was a horse box) had come to a halt and a man and a woman were letting down the back of it.

First of all they manhandled out a powerful-looking white motor-cycle which Simon observed with the proper interest of a fifteen year old in such things; it looked to him like a twin Norton and he would have given a great deal to own it himself.

The man and the woman then went back to the horse box and began to help somebody out of it—a man who from the assistance the others had to give him seemed to be injured or at least in some sort of difficulty.

The boy watched all this uncomprehendingly but with interest; then suddenly the man who had been helping the injured passenger out of the horse box raised his head and looked over to the privet hedge. After a second's hesitation he began to walk slowly in Simon's direction and the boy felt immensely relieved. What problems of their own these people might have he neither knew nor cared about; he fondly imagined that his own troubles had come to an end.

TEN

HOOKY DIDN'T HURRY driving back from the point-to-point. Frequently he enjoyed speed for the sake of speed and would rattle his faithful Jag along at the best pace he could get out of her, but the whole ambience of the afternoon had been so pleasant and the ministrations of Striped Waistcoat so consoling that he was content to go gently over the moorland roads and to take his time about getting back to Sheepsgate.

By no means all of the one hundred and sixty pounds which he had won on Perfect Pest remained. (*The trouble with you, Hooky, is that you never know when to stop* was one of the favourite warnings from the High Priestess of Hove) but on the other hand by no means all of it had vanished and Hooky couldn't help feeling more kindly disposed towards young Simon Loeson. If that youth were not such a bloody little nuisance I would never have backed the horse, he reflected. If he isn't in too irritating a mood I'll give him a fiver for himself.

From thinking about his winnings on Perfect Pest his thoughts turned to the trim, slim figure on Gaiety Girl carrying the white with blue star, the blue and white hooped sleeves so bravely and with such panache over the fences. It was delightful to know that she was going to be in the neighbourhood for some time yet and that he would be seeing her again soon.

All these easy and agreeable thoughts received a severe check when he walked into the farmhouse at Sheepsgate and an angry Rachel met him with 'Do you know what that silly boy has done?' Hooky's heart sank. He had never felt

completely easy about taking the day off, it being a firm
conviction of his that Life always waited until you dropped
your guard and then let you have it on the chin.

'What's happened?' he asked.

'What has happened,' Rachel replied, speaking slowly
and very distinctly as people will when they are angry, 'is
that in spite of all I have said on the subject, and I know you
have backed me up in this, Hooky, because I have heard
you, that conceited young ass has actually saddled up my
mare Cinders and gone out on her.'

'Without your permission?'

'*Of course*, without my permission. I wouldn't dream of
letting him do it. I told him so half a dozen times. Just wait
till he gets back, that's all.'

'How long has he been out?'

'I'm not sure.'

'You didn't see him go?'

'Of course, I didn't see him go. If I had seen him go I
would have stopped him, wouldn't I?'

'Sorry, Rachel, I'm being rather stupid. Of course, you
would have stopped him. Damn the boy. By God, I'll give
him an earful when he comes in.'

'I think he must have gone about three o'clock. Somewhere about then. During the morning he was helping
Francis with the fencing in Little Twitchell, then at lunch he
said he was bored with that and what else was there to do. I
said I was going to be jam-making all afternoon and he
could help me by washing out a whole lot of last year's jars.
It did strike me that he was being rather a long time about
it, but I didn't mind as long as he was kept busy doing
something and wasn't getting under my feet in the kitchen.

'In the middle of the afternoon I began to wonder what
on earth he was doing with the jars—there weren't all that
many to wash anyway—and I went to have a look. The jars
were there, but no Simon. I thought perhaps he had decided to go back to Francis in Little Twitchell; but, of

course, as soon as I went out into the yard I saw the stable door open.'

'And how long ago was that?'

'Well, like I said, the middle of the afternoon; about half past three, I suppose.'

Hooky glanced at his wristwatch.

'So he's been gone two hours?'

'At least. Goodness knows what he's doing to the mare. I don't want her ridden for two hours, and badly ridden at that; I don't suppose Simon's got a clue about how to handle a horse.'

'Do you suppose he'll stick on?'

'Quite likely not. She's a tricky ride, even if you're used to her. Hooky, when that boy comes back you have got to make it absolutely clear to him that if he goes anywhere near the stable again he'll be packing his bags and leaving the same day.'

Hooky nodded. 'When Master Simon comes back,' he said, 'leave him to me. By God, I'll sort the young devil out.'

Half an hour later Rachel, then sitting in the living-room in front of the wood fire, jerked up her head. Her quick ears had been the first to hear the mare's hooves in the yard.

'There they are,' she cried jumping up.

Hooky followed her out, only to find that 'they' were not there after all. The mare was there mud-splashed and with the saddle halfway under her belly. Of her rider there wasn't a sign.

Rachel caught and quietened the mare who was obviously in a highly nervous state and took her into the stable. 'I'll just see that Cinders is all right,' she said, 'and then we'll have to decide what to do.'

The subsequent council of war was held over drinks in the living-room. Rachel spoke first. 'It's pretty obvious he was thrown. Not a clue about how to saddle up, of course, so he didn't get the girths tight enough. The saddle slipped and Cinders wouldn't stand for that, naturally, so she took to her heels and off he came. Thank goodness the mare isn't injured.'

'And what about Simon?'

'Well, he's probably shaken up and scared and is making his painful way back. And I hope it *is* painful for him. I hope his scraped shin or whatever he's got is hurting like hell.'

'Suppose he came off six or seven miles away and doesn't know the way back?' Francis put in.

Rachel shrugged her shoulders.

Hooky could understand Rachel's lack of concern but it was an attitude he couldn't allow himself to adopt.

'Is there any danger of his getting bogged?' he asked.

Francis nodded. 'Yes. Definitely there is. If you don't know your way about and aren't careful there's always the risk of getting into a bad patch, and we've got to think about the light—it will be dark in an hour.'

'I wish to God I'd never gone to the point-to-point,' Hooky said.

'Don't be silly, Hooky,' Rachel chided him. 'It isn't your fault. Even if you hadn't gone the boy would probably have sneaked off just the same.'

'I wonder if the people up at Castlecroft have seen anything of him,' Francis suggested. 'I've not actually met the new man there—'

'I've met him,' Hooky put in, 'in the Huntsman. Berry by name. He seems a reasonable sort of chap.'

'Give him a ring. He'll be under the old number. Twenty-seven I think it is. At least we can ask them to keep a look out and meanwhile you and I had better tour round in the Land Rover, Hooky.'

The telephone call to Exdale 27 was answered promptly.

'Captain Berry here, Castlecroft.'

'My name's Hefferman. I think we've met in the Huntsman. I'm down here—at Sheepsgate actually—writing a book.'

'Ah, yes, I remember. And what can I do for you, Mister—Hefferman, did you say?'

'That's it. We're worried over a youngster....' Hooky detailed the story of Simon Loeson's disappearance, which was listened to, apparently, with solicitous attention.

'So it looks as though the boy is wandering about on the moor?' Berry said when Hooky had finished.

'Unless he's cracked his head on a stone and is lying unconscious somewhere. Anyway, I take it you've seen nothing of him?'

'Not a glimpse. But, of course, we haven't been looking. Now you've told me all this I'll have a word with Mrs Berry and we'll do a bit of scouting round. What's the boy's name again?'

'Simon Loeson.'

'And you are staying where?'

'Next door to you, at Sheepsgate, with Major and Mrs Dobson.'

'Right. Well, of course, if we hear or see anything I'll give you a ring right away, Mr Hefferman.'

'That's kind of you. You'll understand, I'm sure, that with evening coming on we are getting a bit anxious.'

Francis and Rachel had both been standing by Hooky whilst he was telephoning so there was no necessity for him to enlarge on what had been said.

'Well, come on,' Francis said. 'You and I will take a look round in the Land Rover, Hooky. It's a bit of a wild goose chase because the moor's a big place, but you never know, we might strike lucky.'

After an hour and a half they were back and it was dark; night had crept quietly over the moor and laid an obliterating hand on everything. They had not struck lucky.

'Not a sign of anything,' Hooky said in answer to Rachel's enquiring look. 'Not a sausage, not one single sausage. Any joy from the people at Castlecroft?'

'They rang about half an hour ago but they haven't seen anything of him.'

'So now what do we do?'

'Ring the police at Exdale in case Simon has been picked up unconscious and taken into hospital somewhere.'

The Sergeant on the desk at Exdale listened sympathetically and with interest (he was a moorland man) and he promised to make enquiries round the hospitals of the district.

'You've had nothing reported to you yet, Sergeant?'

'Not yet, sir, no. If I was you I'd get on to EMRA. They might not be able to organize anything tonight, but they'd get cracking first thing in the morning.'

'He suggests EMRA,' Francis said putting down the phone, 'and they are the obvious people to help.'

'EMRA?' Hooky queried.

'Exdale Moorland Rescue Association. It's a voluntary set-up. All local people. Young farmers who know the moor mostly and they rope in Boy Scouts and anyone else who will give a hand. When somebody is reported lost they mount a seek-and-find operation. As I say, they know the ground and between them they search it pretty thoroughly.'

Rachel moved to the corner cupboard in the living-room where the drinks were kept. She had got over her anger about the mare being taken out without permission and now her chief feeling was one of sympathy for Hooky.

She produced a bottle of Scotch and poured out three drinks, taking care that Hooky's was an especially generous one.

'Come on, Hooky,' she said. 'I know how you're feeling, but there's absolutely nothing more we can do tonight. I do really assure you that looking for anybody on the moor on a dark night like this is simply hopeless. Francis will get on to the man who runs this EMRA thing in a minute and they'll lay on something for tomorrow. And, you never know, Simon might suddenly turn up yet.'

Hooky did his best to look as though he believed her and accepted his drink with gratitude.

'Not much soda,' he said.

Luckily Francis's telephone call to the organizer of EMRA caught that energetic little man just as he was on the point of leaving home for a darts match at the Huntsman.

'If you'd rung five minutes later I wouldn't have been here, Major.'

'Thank the Lord I caught you.'

'What is it, then?'

Francis explained the situation and EMRA listened carefully. He was an enthusiast. He didn't really care that somebody was lost on the moor. What mattered to him was the fun of the search.

'Any idea what direction he might have gone in, Major?'

'None at all. The boy doesn't know the district. He might have gone anywhere.'

'What about the condition of the mare? Would you say she had gone far?'

'She had obviously galloped quite a bit and she was muddied so she had been through some wet patches; but they could be pretty well anywhere.'

'Let's see, Sheepsgate, aren't you? Who's beyond you? Castlecroft, isn't it?'

'That's right. People called Berry. Newcomers.'

'They've seen nothing?'

'No. I've been on to them. They're doing what they can, keeping a look out and so on; but no joy so far.'

'Right. Well, I'll get cracking straight away. I'll be seeing a couple of my chaps down at the Huntsman at the darts match and they can warn their pals. I expect we can have a search party ready by nine o'clock tomorrow morning. We had better report to your place and work from there. Can you fix coffee for the lads?'

'Yes, of course. How many?'

'I shall try to get a dozen, and that's not a lot to look for anything on the moor, as you know.'

Francis replaced the telephone and turned to the others. 'Well, that's something,' he said. 'EMRA will have a search party of a dozen up here tomorrow by nine o'clock, and incidentally they'll all want coffee, Rachel.'

'They can have anything they want as long as they find that silly boy,' Rachel assured him.

Hooky glanced at the clock. The evening was slipping by and it was getting more and more difficult to retain any belief in Rachel's optimistic statement that 'Simon might suddenly turn up'. The idea of telephoning to Charles Wilbury was not one that appealed to Hooky but he realized that he would have to face it.

The bell rang in the cubby hole of the hall in the Timmerton Square flat and Charles Wilbury went to answer it in great good humour. The man of law was feeling in fine form. The pressures of the Loeson affair had been considerably easier for the last few days, and the firm of accountants who looked after the financial side of Oldmeadow, Williams & Wilbury had weighed in with an extremely satisfactory report. Add to this the fact that he was bidden later that evening to a supper party at the New Berkley at which at least two peers would be present and anyone who knew Charles would readily understand the almost exuberant voice in which he said, 'Hallo, Charles Wilbury here, Timmerton Square.'

He had been wondering if and when a report of how things were going down at Sheepsgate would be made so he was not altogether surprised to hear Hooky's voice.

He was not prepared, however, for Hooky's news, to which he listened with an ever-increasing look of dismay on his features.

'But God almighty, Hefferman, are you telling me the boy has vanished?'

'I'm telling you that the boy did what he has been told fifty times not to do—took Rachel Dobson's horse out without permission; he was obviously thrown from it and he must be either wandering about lost or lying out hurt somewhere.'

'But damn it you must *do* something—'

'Listen, Wilbury; Dobson and I have been out looking; the people from the neighbouring property have been out looking; we've rung up the police, and a local rescue association are going to have a dozen people out tomorrow searching—what more can we do?'

'He went out riding on Mrs Dobson's horse, you say?'

'She thought he was in one of the outhouses washing out jam-jars or some such chore he had undertaken to do; and apparently he just went into the stable, saddled up (which incidentally he made a balls of) and rode off.'

'Where were you?'

'About fifteen miles away at an entertainment known as a point-to-point, winning money.'

'Mr Loeson won't like that.'

'Ring him up and tell him everything.'

'I can't, thank God—not at once, anyway. He's not in the country. At this moment he's in a jet on his way to Johannesburg.'

'Can you get in touch with him, then?'

'I don't know that I can. Not easily, certainly. And I hope I don't have to; surely to God you'll find the boy tomorrow, won't you?'

'We'll all do our damnedest, I can promise you that.'

EMRA was as good as its word; rather better in fact, for shortly after nine next morning no fewer than fourteen people were assembled in front of the house at Sheepsgate. Six of them were on horseback; the remaining eight had come in a variety of cars. The energetic, bustling little man in charge obviously knew the drill and had the whole operation thoroughly organized. After hearing once again from the Dobsons and Hooky all that they had to say, maps (two-and-a-half-inch Ordnance) of the moor were consulted and different areas for searching apportioned to different groups of the party.

'If you find anything let me know on your walkie-talkie,' the little man ordered. 'And in any case report back here by five o'clock. Any questions? O.K., then, off you go.'

The walkie-talkie outfits, the first-aid kits that were carried, and above all the obvious air of general efficiency were all impressive and Hooky felt heartened.

'With this lot you're sure to find him, aren't you?' he asked.

The organizer made a grimace; in private conversation he sounded a lot less confident than when giving out his orders.

'The moor's a tricky old place,' he warned. 'You can look till your eyes fall out but you can still miss a lot. Still, the lads will do their best, I can promise you that.'

Hooky and Francis went out on a search of their own all morning but came back empty-handed at lunch-time. Rachel had only to look at their faces to know the answer to the question she inevitably asked.

'Not a sign of the boy,' Francis said. 'Still, EMRA may have better luck.'

There was still the fencing job in Little Twitchell to be completed, and in order to take his mind off other matters Hooky volunteered to give Francis a hand with it.

'Cheer up, Hooky; no good moping,' Francis urged him.

Hooky agreed. Moping never did anybody any good, and he was not by nature a moper. All the same he was finding it very hard to be cheerful.

'What the hell happens to people on the moor?' he demanded. 'How can anyone just vanish?'

'All too easily, I'm afraid. If you're not used to the look of the ground and start striding out straight across country regardless you can find yourself up to your middle in bog before you know what's hit you.'

'And then what happens?'

'If you're lucky and you know the drill you can probably get yourself back on to firm ground.'

'And if not?'

Francis made a face and bent down to pick up a length of new railing.

'And if not?' Hooky insisted.

'Damn it, Hooky, don't go on asking. Bog can be desperately dangerous stuff. If you panic and start threshing about like mad, which most people do instinctively, the odds are you'll find yourself getting further and further in; of course, you shout like hell, but the moor isn't what you would call thickly populated and if there's no one to hear and help you. . . .' He shrugged his shoulders.

'You think that's what happened?'

'I think that the EMRA people know the moor like nobody else does, and that by five o'clock this afternoon they'll be back here with some good news for us. Now, come on, get hold of this rail and let's get on with the fencing.'

By shortly after five the different EMRA search parties were all back and had handed in their Ordnance maps and their reports to the organizer. Rachel had tea ready for all of them and they were obviously glad of it but there was nothing they could give in return.

'Not a sign anywhere' was the verdict.

'But the boy has got to be *somewhere*,' Hooky insisted.

EMRA spread his hands. 'He takes a toss off the horse, hits his head on a stone and can't do any better than crawl along a bit before he flakes out. So there he is lying unconscious in the bracken somewhere and, unless anybody searching is lucky enough to stumble over him, mighty difficult to see.'

All this was poor comfort for Hooky and at half past six Rachel gave him his orders.

'Hooky, there is absolutely nothing more that you or any of us can do this evening. If any telephone call comes through from the police, or anywhere, Francis and I will be here to deal with it. What you have got to do is to get into that marvellous Jag of yours and take yourself off to the Huntsman in Exdale; and Hooky—'

'Ma'am?'

'Half what you feel like drinking will probably be enough.'

It was very seldom that Hooky took orders from anybody about his drinking habits, but this time he nodded submissively.

'Entendu,' he said, 'and in case you don't know that's a French phrase meaning you are a remarkable woman.'

Rachel smiled at him.

Only the Archdeacon behind the bar was in the Huntsman when Hooky when in. A radio set was giving out news and there was just time to catch something about 'off the moor' before the Archdeacon switched off.

'What was that about the moor?' Hooky demanded eagerly.

'Good evening, sir. It was a news item relating to the prisoner who escaped from Dartmoor yesterday. It seems that the white motor-cycle on which he got away has been found abandoned in the car-park at Exeter Station.'

Hooky was not interested in white motor-cycles, escaping prisoners or Dartmoor. Exmoor was occupying his thoughts to the exclusion of pretty well all else.

'Shall I mix you your usual Pimms, sir?'

Hooky was on the point of answering when the door opened and he waited to see who was coming in; then—

'Make it two,' he ordered as Fenella entered, 'make it two.'

She was slim and trim, wearing the sort of tweeds which even today a woman can only get cut in London; she was a sight for sore eyes.

'Am I glad to see you,' Hooky said. 'Seeing you is the first nice thing that has happened in the last twenty-four hours.'

She shot a quick look at him; the soldier of fortune sounded at odds with life.

'Whatever's the matter, Hooky?' she asked.

'Wait till we get our Pimms and I'll tell you the whole sad story.' The Archdeacon ceremoniously presented the tall glasses festooned with herbs and fruit.

'I hear you rode a very good race at the point-to-point yesterday, miss,' he said.

'Not as good as all that, I'm afraid. I only came in third.'

'His Grace wasn't one for what nowadays they call women's lib, but he always used to say that any lady who rode in a point-to-point race should be given a medal for pluck.'

'You can say that again,' Hooky agreed. 'Nothing would get me riding in one again and incidentally I wish I'd never gone to the meeting yesterday.'

'I thought you won handsomely on Perfect Pest?' Fenella said in surprise.

'So I did; but, listen....'

He related his tale of woe and at the conclusion of it Fenella said briskly, 'Well, the stupid boy has gone and got himself lost. I can't see that you are to blame.'

'If I had been there it wouldn't have happened.'

'Nobody could expect you never to take a day off.'

'I can just imagine what my aunt would say about this.'

'You've got an aunt, Hooky?'

'The old lady is not so much an aunt as the quintessence of Auntism. She's formidable and I'm terrified of her.'

Fenella put her head back and laughed merrily.

'What's so funny?' Hooky demanded sourly.

'I can't imagine you being terrified of anything or anybody.'

'You haven't seen my Aunt Theresa.'

'Come on, Hooky, snap out of it.'

'Yes, I know there's nothing more depressing than a dismal Jimmy. Sorry, Fen, you are quite right. It's the feeling of *helplessness* that's so frustrating. The boy must be out there somewhere, in a comparatively small area actually, and we just can't find him.'

'And you say the people at the next farm—what's it called? Castlecroft?—haven't seen anything?'

'Not a thing.'

'What sort of people are they? Helpful and sympathetic and so on?'

'On the phone the man naturally said he would keep an eye open, but of course it isn't their worry really. I'm not looking forward to telling the boy's father, Loeson; my God, he'll be unpleasant about it. I tell you what, Fen. I've more than half a mind to give up the private-eye business after this lot.'

'Oh, Hooky, I should have thought it was tremendous fun.'

Hooky made a face. 'Pretty seedy and tawdry a lot of it,' he said. 'I think I'll retire to the country and raise chickens.'

Fenella caught the Archdeacon's eye.

'Mr Hefferman is getting maudlin,' she said. 'May we have another issue of rejuvenating medicine, please?'

The Archdeacon smiled affably; he had a soft spot in his heart for high-spirited young ladies.

'Two more Pimms, miss,' he said. 'Certainly.'

ELEVEN

SIMON WAS SITTING up in bed when Berry entered the room.

'How are you feeling this morning?' Berry asked with a great show of affability.

Simon, who didn't like many grown-ups, certainly didn't like this one; he was much too hearty and 'old-fellowish' for Simon's taste.

'My shoulder still hurts a bit.'

'Of course it does, old fellow, of course it does. Sure to. You must have taken a nasty tumble.'

'Is a doctor coming to see me?'

'Well, I don't know that you actually need a doctor. After all, there's nothing broken is there? Mrs Berry knows a lot about nursing and she's had a good look at it. She says it's just a question of resting it for three or four days in bed and then you'll be as right as rain.'

'Is that what Major and Mrs Dobson say too?'

'Oh, yes, they agree absolutely.'

'You've told them I'm here, haven't you?'

'Of course we have, old fellow. What do you think?'

'And Mr Hefferman, he knows as well?'

'Everybody knows.'

'I suppose Mrs Dobson's angry about my taking her horse out, is she?'

'I wouldn't worry about that.'

'I honestly don't want to stay in bed three or four days; I'm sure I shall be all right tomorrow.'

'We'll see how you are after today.'

'Why should I stay in bed if I don't want to?'

A little of the affability began to fade from Captain Berry's manner.

'I'm afraid you'll have to do as you're told for a bit,' he said.

'I shall be all right tomorrow and then I can go back to Sheepsgate, can't I?'

'We'll see about that. We'll see how you're feeling.'

'Has my father been told about this?'

'Your father? I don't know about that. I expect Mr Hefferman will have phoned him.'

'I should like to phone him.'

'Not for a bit. You won't be getting up for twenty-four hours or so.'

'Why not, if I wake up tomorrow feeling all right?'

'Listen,' Berry's voice hardened suddenly. 'You'll get up when you are told you can and not before, so stop bothering about it.'

He went out of the bedroom and Simon was left to look for a few minutes at a book which he wasn't interested in and then aimlessly to count the clusters of roses in a repetitive wallpaper pattern. His mind went back to the events of the previous afternoon; he remembered the feeling of intense relief that had swept over him when he had gained the crest on which the three windswept trees stood and had suddenly seen the house and buildings in front of him. Not only a house and buildings, but people. The white motorcycle and the man being helped out of the horse box.... Then the other man, the one he had learned to call Captain Berry, had looked up suddenly and seen him standing there by the privet hedge. Berry had come over to him and asked in low, angry tones, 'Who the hell are you?' He was angry because he was badly scared; the one thing that Big Boy didn't want had happened—*publicity*, somebody knew.

'Who the hell are you?'

There could be no mistaking the fright-inspired venom in the words, and Simon didn't like the man from that first moment. He gave an account of what had happened to him and the listening man's attitude began to change visibly. By the time Simon's story was finished Berry was sympathizing with him and saying 'Bad luck, old fellow. Well, we must look after you, mustn't we'; and Simon didn't like that much either.

Now, lying in bed, he wondered who the man was who had been helped out of the horse box and where he had gone to.

Downstairs Berry said, 'The kid's starting to moan about being in bed; says he wants to get up tomorrow for certain.'

'Well, he can't.'

'Obviously. But it will be difficult to explain to him why not. He says if his shoulder's bad why don't we get a doctor to him.'

Betty lit a cigarette and flicked the match into the fire.

'I wish to God we had never let ourselves get mixed up in this business,' she said.

'We didn't have much option.'

'You didn't have to say "yes" to Big Boy.'

'No?' Berry gave a dry laugh. 'Things have a way of happening to people who say "no" to Big Boy. And anyway there's five thousand in it for us, don't forget.'

'I just hope we get it and can clear out of the country for a bit, that's all. I don't see how we can be blamed for what happened. After all, we didn't know the boy was going to be out riding and would have an accident, did we?'

'Oh, be your age, Betty, for God's sake. What's the sense in talking like that? The whole essence of the thing was nobody knowing about it. Everything Big Boy planned went perfectly; the explosion and the getaway and the motor-cycle business; and then at this end there's an inquisitive fifteen-year-old kid watching it all. You can't expect Big Boy to be pleased about that.'

'I have never been more astonished in my life than when we were helping Lenny out of the horse box and something made me look up and I saw the boy standing there watching us. I mean we are so off the map in this Godforsaken place nobody ever does come here, do they?'

'Not much good trying to explain to Big Boy that something never happens when in point of fact it *has* happened.'

'So what do we do next?'

'Play it by ear as we go along. That's all we can do. We can fool the kid that he's got to stay in bed for a couple of days more anyway.'

'And after that?'

'I suppose we shall get instructions from London. But obviously Big Boy can't afford to turn this kid loose and let him go back to his friends; after all, he saw us getting Lenny and the motor-cycle out of the horse box. My guess is that a car will be sent down here and the kid will be taken up to London.'

'And what will happen to him up there?'

Berry shrugged his shoulders. 'That won't be our worry. That won't be anything to do with us.'

The woman threw her half-smoked cigarette into the fire. 'Like I said a moment ago,' she repeated, 'I wish to God we had never got mixed up in it.'

Lying in bed Simon took to counting the rosebuds on the wallpaper again; he wondered what Hooky Hefferman and the Dobsons were saying about him; something pretty uncomplimentary he imagined, and the thought amused him; he was not a boy who cared about how much trouble he caused to other people. He shifted his position and moved his right arm and shoulder a little; there was still some stiffness and soreness there but he didn't believe it was bad enough to keep him in bed. *You'll get up when you're told you can and not before, so stop bothering*. He hadn't liked the tone of that. I'll ring up home tonight, he thought, and tell Pop everything that's happened and tell him I want to go back to Hampstead.

Presently he got out of bed and went down the corridor to the bathroom at the end of it. He used the lavatory and then washed in the basin. Whilst he was drying his hands he looked out of the window and saw the woman of the house crossing the yard towards the stable. He was surprised to see that she was carrying a tray with plates and food on it. She took this into the stable and Simon stood at the bathroom window waiting for her to come out; when she hadn't done so after a few minutes he turned and went back to the bedroom, wondering.

LENNY WAS SITTING on a bale of straw smoking and looking at the day's newspaper which he had read through twice already.

'For God's sake be careful with that cigarette,' the woman said when she appeared with his meal on a tray. 'I don't like smoking in a stable.'

'Don't worry; I'll be careful. I won't set fire to anything. I've got quite enough to think about without burning everything up. What's the news?'

'Nothing fresh. They found the motor-cycle in the station car-park in Exeter, but you knew that last night; so presumably they will think you have made it up to London.'

'They may do. But the Law isn't as stupid as people say. They may read it right and think it's a blind and keep on looking in this part of the world. What did Big Boy say on the blower?'

'Lie low and do nothing till we get further orders.'

'And what about the boy?'

'He's in bed and we'll have to keep him there.'

'Is he hurt?'

'Not really. Not injured.'

'So what about when he wants to get up and go back home or wherever it was he came from?'

'We shan't be able to let him, that's all.'

'By God, you two made a right mess of things, not making sure there was nobody about when I arrived.'

'I know we did. No point in rubbing it in. I wish to Heaven it was all finished with.'

'Me too. You don't imagine I'm enjoying being shut up here, do you?'

'It's better than Dartmoor.'

'Just,' Lenny agreed grudgingly.

In point of fact the strange psychological truth was that he was finding being shut away in the loft of Castlecroft rather more irksome than being in prison. His getaway had succeeded brilliantly and the excitement of it had been intense and now everything had fizzled out to confinement again, and confinement with even less movement and fewer contacts than he had enjoyed in Dartmoor. There were good points about it, of course; the food for one thing. Betty had never claimed to be more than averagely good at cooking, but after what he had been used to in prison the meals she prepared tasted like something out of the *Good Food Guide*. He studied her for a moment as she bent to put the tray down on a second bale of hay that served as a table.

'Three Fingers' Lenny had been without a woman for a considerable time and the closeness of this one, up in the loft alone with him, was disturbing. The strange but undeniable telepathy which makes a woman aware that a man is thinking about her touched Betty. She put the tray of food in position and straightened up.

'I suppose it's pretty grim in there?' she asked looking curiously at the man.

'It was pretty grim looking forward to twenty-five years of it. Christ, twenty-five years. I'd be sixty when I came out!'

'What was the worst of it—no women?'

'The old timers say you get used to that. I wasn't there long enough to know, thank God.'

'And you're going back to London?'

'I'll be back in the Smoke as soon as Big Boy gives me the nod. What about you?'

'I'm not sure yet.'

'You'll be staying on down here?'

'Not down here, no. We'll be moving somewhere.'

'Who's we? Just you and your husband? Is he your husband by the way?'

'We're married, yes.'

Lenny grinned. 'Like that, is it?' he asked.

The woman turned away. 'You'd better have your breakfast, Lenny,' she said, 'and I'll go into the house. Berry will be wondering what's become of me.'

When she got back into the house Berry asked, 'Everything O.K.?'

'Perfectly. He's bored, that's all.'

'Bored? My God, that's rich. He'd be a damned sight more bored in Dartmoor.'

'That's what I told him—more or less.'

'At midday I'm going to take a quick run into Exdale. I want to hear if any gossip or rumours are going about; and if that chap Hefferman is there so much the better; if we meet and talk naturally there won't be any suspicions raised and there might be if I faded off the scene completely and shut myself up here.'

Betty nodded. 'Seems sensible,' she agreed.

'I shan't be away more than an hour or an hour and a half at the most. Can you cope?'

'Yes, of course.'

'You had better take the kid a meal about twelve. Eating it will give him something to do. Got any Cokes in the house?'

'Coca-colas? Yes, half a dozen at least. Why?'

'Give him one with his lunch and slip one of my yellow sleeping-tablets in it. That will make him drowsy most of the afternoon.'

Simon heard a car engine start up outside and moved out
of bed to the window. This time it wasn't the horse box but
Captain Berry driving off in the Land Rover. The boy was
still at the window when the door of his bedroom opened
and the woman came in carrying a tray. Betty wasn't good
with youngsters; she did her best to sound friendly, but her
efforts didn't make much impression on Simon.

'You ought not to be out of bed, Simon, with that shoulder of yours.'

'Why not? There's nothing much wrong with it.'

'Let's have a look at it and see.'

Reluctantly the boy submitted himself for inspection. He
was wearing a pair of Berry's pyjamas which were far too
big for him. The woman looked at his shoulder, fingering it
in what she hoped was a knowing manner. She had in fact
done a course of first aid at one time in her life and was not
entirely without rudimentary knowledge.

'Well, there's nothing broken anyway,' she said.

'Of course there isn't. We know that. It's just a bit painful, that's all.'

'Give it a rest for a couple more days and you'll be all
right.'

'I'm all right now. What about my clothes; when can I
have those back?'

'They're still drying. You must have been right up to your
middle in that bog.'

'They've been drying all night.'

'I'll have a look at them this afternoon and see if the mud
will brush off. I've brought your lunch, Simon. Hungry?'

'Yes I am.'

'Do you like Coke?'

'Coke? Yes I do.'

'Good. I've brought one up for you on your tray.'

'Who was that other tray for?'

'What other tray?'

'The one you were carrying into the stable.'

'How do you know I was carrying anything into the stable?'

'I saw you from the bathroom window. I was going to the loo.'

'We've got someone doing some work for us out there.'

'Is that the man I saw yesterday?'

'What man? No, it isn't. It's nothing to do with you, Simon; just a workman doing a job in the stable. Now get on with your lunch and drink up your Coke and have a good sleep this afternoon; you'll feel all the better for it.'

'And then I can telephone home this evening, can't I?'

'Telephone home? You mean the people at Sheepsgate?'

'No, home. My father. In London.'

'I—I don't know about that. I'm not sure you will be able to.'

'Why not?'

'Well, for one thing we've been having trouble with the phone. At the moment it's out of order.'

'Is it?'

When the woman got back into the kitchen she hesitated there only a few moments and then went out of the back door and crossed the yard towards the stable. Halfway across the yard she turned and looked up at the bathroom window. Nobody was watching her. As she entered the stable itself and began to climb up the vertical wall-ladder into the loft she told herself: I'm going to see Lenny because of the boy; he's getting too suspicious and Lenny ought to be told; that's why I'm going.

He looked up when she entered his hiding-place at the end of the loft and smiled. He didn't seem surprised to see her.

'Any news? Anything fresh?' he asked automatically.

'The boy's getting suspicious; he's been asking questions.'

'Tell the little sod to keep his mouth shut.'

'He's been asking questions about you.'

'What's Berry say about it?'

'Berry's away at the moment. In Exdale.'

Lenny looked at her and his smile increased. 'Your hus-and's gone to Exdale?' he asked.

'He wants to see if there are any rumours going around bout whether you really got away to London or are still omewhere in the West Country, and also he thinks it bet-r to keep up his usual habits and be seen as usual in the ub and so on.'

Lenny nodded approval. 'Very wise, I'd say. How long is e likely to be gone?'

Betty dodged that question. 'What are we going to do bout the boy, Lenny?' she asked. 'He wants to telephone is home now.'

'Well, for Christ's sake, he can't telephone home. He an't telephone anybody. You understand that, don't you? ou never ought to have let him be here at all and now ou're talking about letting him telephone—'

'No I'm not. I told him he couldn't phone. I told him the hone was out of order. He'll be all right this afternoon nyway. I gave him a Coke with his lunch and put one of erry's sleeping-tablets in it. He'll be asleep for three or four ours at least.'

'He'll be asleep for a damned sight longer if he gets in Big oy's way, I can tell you. What's up? What are you going r?'

'I don't know how long Berry will be away. He might just ook in at the Exdale pub and come straight back.'

'Will he be going there again tomorrow?'

'He might do.'

'You could tell him it's a sensible thing to do, couldn't ou? You could tell him everything would be all right here hilst he's away. Everything would be fine.'

The woman gave a ghost of a smile. 'Yes, I expect I could ll him that,' she agreed, but nevertheless she turned and ent out of that small confined space. She was trembling ightly; there was something about Lenny (the fact that he

was an ex-prisoner, and a known man of violence?) th
disturbed her profoundly.

Shortly after five o'clock that afternoon the telephor
rang in the Castlecroft living-room and Betty answered
The first words she heard made the expression on her fa
change quickly. She put a hand over the receiver and sa
across the room to her husband,

'Big Boy. He wants to speak to you. Christ, I hate th
man.'

Berry was beginning to hate Big Boy too, but he didr
think it wise to advertise the fact.

'Everything O.K. here,' he led off cheerfully. 'Nothing
worry about.'

'Don't sound so bloody bright, for God's sake, not aft
the cock-up you made of things. What do you mean not
ing to worry about? There's plenty to worry about. I'll t
you when to stop worrying. How's Lenny?'

'That's what I mean. Lenny's all right. Perfectly. Just
bit browned off at being hidden away, that's all.'

'You tell him from me, *from me*, to keep hidden. N
poking his head out to have a look round or any nonsen
like that. Got it?'

'Yes.'

'And another thing; don't let him see any women. Le
ny's a terror with women.'

'There aren't any round here, only just ourselves.'

'Any sign of the Law?'

'No. Nobody's been around. Nobody at all.'

'What about the boy?'

'He's in bed at the moment, but—'

'But what? I don't want any "buts".'

'We can't keep him in bed indefinitely, can we?'

'Anyone been looking for him?'

'Nobody's been here. They rang up and asked if we ha
seen anything of him and of course I said no but we'd ke

ur eyes open; and they've had people all over the moor
earching.'

'Are they still looking?'

'Sure to be. They'll keep it up for maybe another couple
f days and then they'll assume he got bogged and is done
or and they'll give it up. The trouble is the boy's getting
estless, he wants to know can he telephone his father.'

'For Christ's sake, Berry, what's the matter with you?
estless? What the hell do you mean restless, a kid of fif-
en?'

'I'm only just telling you—'

'No, listen, *I'm* telling *you*. And I don't often tell people
ings twice; it isn't my way. Don't let that kid go anywhere
ear a telephone. Don't let him get near anything. Got it?'

'Yes. O.K.'

'You can tell Lenny the Law has been ferreting about
ound his old haunts up in Newington Road and they've got
omebody watching the house where that black woman he
sed to go with lives. But whether they really think he's in
e Smoke or not I don't know. You can tell him I'm aim-
g to get him up to Newcastle and across by boat to Nor-
ay. It isn't fixed but I think I can work it.'

'O.K. I'll tell him. And what about the boy?'

'Watch him. If he's got to be fixed, I'll see to it. Mean-
hile, as far as you are concerned, *watch him*. Maybe I'll
ome down there and have a look at things myself before
ou foul anything else up.'

Berry put the telephone down and Betty looked at him
nquiringly.

'Well, you heard what I said so you can pretty well guess
hat he was on about. He says he may be coming down here
mself.'

'I hope to God he doesn't. And what about the boy up-
airs?'

'For the time being keep him.'

'I suppose we can manage it for a day or two.'

'We've got to.'

'What did he say about Lenny?'

'He's going to try to get him up to Newcastle and acr⟨ to Norway from there. He also gave me a warning.'

'What kind of a warning?'

'Apparently Lenny's a bit of a terror with women.'

Betty moved over to the drinks table and began to p⟨ whisky into a glass.

'I wonder what he means by that,' she said.

'Well, if you can't guess you haven't got much imagi⟨ tion. Pour one for me, will you? I feel I want something ⟨ ter talking to that man.'

Whilst Betty was dealing with the drinks the teleph⟨ rang again. 'O.K.,' Berry said, 'I'll take it.'

Upstairs in the small bedroom Simon woke drows⟨ hovering for several minutes in the uncertain world of se⟨ conscious. When he finally became fully aware of thin⟨ latched on to the stream of consciousness, knew that he ⟨ Simon Loeson, remembered where he was and how he ⟨ come to be there—when all this had fallen into place ag⟨ he stretched out his hand to the clock at his bedside ⟨ consulted it. He was astonished to discover that the time ⟨ already well after five. He couldn't remember having sl⟨ through a whole afternoon before and he supposed it m⟨ be the unusual sleep that made his throat feel dry and ⟨ head muzzy.

He sat up in bed and began to speculate about his cloth⟨ The woman had said she would look at them in the af⟨ noon to see if they were dry. He wondered if she had d⟨ so; and suddenly *he wondered something else—he w⟨ dered if she had really meant to do it*. He didn't know ⟨ actly how or why the thought had come into his head; ⟨ there it was; and it frightened him. The boy was sudde⟨ invaded by a feeling that somehow everything was all wro⟨ that even when he felt perfectly well and able to get up ⟨ wasn't going to be allowed to.

It didn't make sense and he tried to tell himself so and that therefore he mustn't believe it; but then a lot of things didn't make sense. Carrying a meal on a tray out to the stables didn't make much sense even if you did have a workman doing a job there; surely it would be more sensible to ask the workman into the kitchen.

He decided to go down the corridor to the loo again and when he was there he took a long look out of the window. There was no sign of any activity; the stable door was shut and nobody was carrying trays about. He came out of the bathroom and stood for a moment, irresolute, in the corridor.

Beyond the bathroom at the extreme end of the passage there was a door which he had hardly noticed before. After a moment's indecision the boy took the few steps that brought him up to the door and tentatively tried the handle.

It turned and he half-opened the door.

It gave onto what was obviously a flight of back stairs. He could hear somebody talking and he stood there, head cocked on one side, listening, straining to catch what was being said.

Very quietly he went down half a dozen steps to a half-landing and now he could hear a good deal better. The voice was coming up from the living-room below. The man was talking and there were odd pauses in what he was saying which could only mean one thing—he was talking on the telephone. '...No, I'm afraid not.... Of course you are, very worried indeed; I can see that.... Not a sign of him, I'm afraid.... Yes, naturally we will.... Well, we can only hope that you have some luck and find the boy somewhere.... Not at all; naturally we will do all we can to help....'

There was a faint tinkle as the receiver was replaced and after waiting for a few more seconds Simon, now treading very cautiously indeed, made his way up the back stairs and along the landing to his bedroom.

He sat on the bed now thoroughly scared. As soon as the woman came up he was going to say again that he wanted to telephone his father; but he didn't think he was going to be allowed to; he thought he would be told once more that the telephone was out of order. He hadn't quite believed it the first time and now he knew it wasn't true.

TWELVE

BIG BOY'S STATEMENT that he might come down to Castle-croft and have a look at things for himself was unwelcome news.

'For Pete's sake stop saying you wish we had never got mixed up in it,' Berry snapped angrily. 'We *are* mixed up in it and we're going to clear five thousand quid out of it. Very nice too.'

'If we get it.'

'We shall get it all right. That's one good thing about Big Boy—he pays. Have we got any vodka in the house?'

'I don't think so. Plenty of Scotch; but I don't think there's any vodka. Why?'

'It's his tipple. He always drank it at the One-O-One. I had better go into Exdale in the morning and get a couple of bottles.'

'Will Big Boy take Lenny back with him when he goes?'

'God knows. I hope so. I want to be shot of the whole affair just as much as you do. Let Big Boy take charge of Lenny and get him off our hands, don't you agree?'

'Of course. Why should I want to keep Lenny here?'

The following morning, therefore, Berry went into Exdale in the Land Rover and parked it in Turnabout Street. He saw the by now well-known Jag already standing outside the Huntsman so was not surprised to find its owner inside.

Normally Rachel made one shopping expedition a week into the little moorland town, but this particular week she had drawn up her list, armed Hooky with it and the household purse, and sent him off in her stead.

'It's not the slightest use hanging about here and being miserable, Hooky.'

'But I might be looking—'

'You have looked. We've all looked. Four EMRA men are still looking. Much better for you to get away from it for a bit. You can go out searching again when you get back. And anyway I want my shopping done.'

Inside the Huntsman and under the sympathetic eye of the Archdeacon Hooky was somewhat anxiously checking the contents of a large basket against the items on Rachel's neatly written list.

'Two brown loaves; one Madeira cake; large packet of cornflakes; rice; tea; large tin of coffee; butter; lump sugar; three tins of sardines; one oven-ready chicken—damn it, I feel like a perambulating supermarket.'

'You seem to have had a highly successful expedition, if I may say so, sir. I'm sure Mrs Dobson will be grateful to you.'

'And one toilet roll,' Hooky added coming to the end of his purchases. 'I was told to get two, but they would only let me have one.'

'"The art of our necessities is strange that can make vile things precious." *Lear*, sir. There's usually something apt in Shakespeare. May I enquire how your own book is progressing?'

'At the moment the complicated machinery of invention lacks the encouragement of lubrication,' Hooky answered. 'Chu Lung, a Chinese philosopher of some distinction. I don't say he is quite in the same class as Mr W.S. but occasionally he hits the nail on the head.'

The Archdeacon, a specialist in lubrication, was already expertly assembling the ingredients of a Pimms Number One. It was at this stage of the proceedings that Berry came on the scene and Hooky, a convivial creature who disliked drinking alone, immediately invited him to join the party.

'No news of that boy from your place, I suppose?' Berry asked solicitously.

Hooky made a Gallic gesture of helplessness and defeat.

'The trouble is we don't really know where to look. We don't know how far he went on the horse. Presumably it took fright at something and ran away with him; and at some stage off the silly sod came. But that might have been within a mile of the house, or, as far as I can see, it might equally well have been ten miles away.'

'What sort of boy is he?' asked Berry who was enjoying himself.

'Knows it all. And the trouble is that these damned youngsters today *do* know a lot. Most of them are halfway to being Senior Wranglers by the time they reach the sixth form.'

'You think he's resourceful?'

'I hope so. Apparently you've got to be pretty resourceful to get yourself out of a bog if you happen to stumble into one—or so people who know the moor say. I can believe that; but even so it seems to me mighty odd that with the amount of searching we've done there hasn't been a sign of anything. It seems that on the moor it's possible just to vanish.'

The Archdeacon who had been listening to the conversation pointed out that the convict who had escaped from the working party on Dartmoor also seemed to have vanished pretty successfully. 'But I expect they'll get him in the end,' he added.

'What makes you say that?' Berry asked.

'I've always understood that it's very hard for a man to get away from Dartmoor. In the end the moor beats them, so everybody says.'

'But this chap *has* got away. They found his motor-bike at Exeter station.'

'Unless that's a blind,' Hooky put in.

Berry laughed. 'Why should you think it's a blind?' he asked. 'You can bet he went like a bat out of Hell to Exeter and jumped on the first train he could catch. The one thing he would want to do would be to get clear.'

'I can't say I blame him for that,' Hooky said. 'I wonder what sort of chap he is? Must be a pretty tough egg, I imagine.'

'Tough as hell I should think,' Berry agreed. 'All these old lags are. They don't get any sympathy from me, I can tell you.'

'I've always a sneaking bit of sympathy for anybody or anything that's being hunted,' Hooky said. 'Villains, of course, but when a villain is on the run and the whole established machinery is working hard trying to corner him— well, I don't know, you can't help wishing him luck in a way.'

'You probably wouldn't wish villains luck if you knew anything about them,' Berry said virtuously.

'Depends of the villain. There are different sorts and degrees. In private-eye work you come across every kind of variation.'

'In private-eye work?' Berry queried sharply. 'Have you done any of that?'

'Odds and ends. Bits and pieces. Here and there.'

'But are you telling me that you are on a private-eye job down here?'

'Not really. More of a holiday. Keeping an eye on that boy. Nursemaiding. And a right damned good mess I've made of that.'

'Well, you do surprise me,' Berry said easily. 'I thought you were writing a book.'

'Intermittently.'

'Although I must say I never did think that you looked like an author.'

'I haven't got that lean and hungry look that comes from trying to live on your royalties,' Hooky said. 'Though, come to think of it, which of us does look like what he really is?'

'Maybe it's just as well we don't,' Berry laughed, much amused at the idea. 'You ought to go down to Dartmoor and give them a hand there.'

'I've quite enough to worry about here at the moment, thank you. Still, you can't help being interested in whether or not they catch the chap. It was such an ingenious scheme that you find yourself half-wanting him to get away with it.'

'Excuse me interrupting, sir,' the Archdeacon put in, 'but I should like to make it clear that I don't in the least want the man to get away with it. Maybe I'm old-fashioned but to me a bomb is a wicked thing to use. It killed one completely innocent man and it might easily have killed four or five others. His Grace always used to say that half the trouble in the world came from not calling things by their right names and I say the proper name for that is murder.'

Hooky stood rebuked. 'You've got a point there,' he admitted. 'A bomb isn't a pretty thing. I wonder how they got it into the hut.'

'A bag of gellymix wouldn't be all that big,' Berry said.

'Gellymix? Is that what they used?'

For a moment Berry was slightly disconcerted. 'I think that's what I read in one of the papers,' he answered. 'Personally I wouldn't know, of course.'

The Archdeacon caught Hookey's eye. 'I think you may be wanting to order another Pimms, sir,' he suggested.

Hooky glanced towards the door and saw why. 'You are absolutely and entirely right,' he agreed. 'One of your nicest Pimms for Miss D'Aubiac.'

Truth to tell, Hooky was a little surprised to find how glad he was to see that trim, gay figure come in. Light and laughter seemed to come in with her. Hooky's heart (that old reprobate of a thing) was strangely moved at the sight. Hooky remonstrated with the wayward thing: *Heart,* he said, *you're old and tarnished and fretted by experience; you ought to know better;* but his heart didn't believe a word of it: *I'm rejuvenated,* it assured him, *and everything is fresh and new; she's like springtime and the morning of things all over again; nothing could feel less fretted than I do at the moment.*

'Your Pimms, Miss,' the Archdeacon said. Fenella wanted to hear Hooky's news but she refused to let him be downcast about it.

'Hooky, you old sinner, you enjoy being miserable,' she accused him.

'Quite right, I do. As you rapidly approach dissolution and decay being miserable about everything is one of life's greatest pleasures.'

Fenella laughed happily and Hooky's stupid old heart was uplifted by the sound.

'I can quite believe you are dissolute,' she said, 'but you're not decayed yet and it's no good acting as though you were. I don't want to hear any more about that wretched boy until you find him.'

'If we ever do.'

'Hooky, if nobody ever does find him it won't be your fault. Tell me one thing, though, about the horse—was that hurt in any way?'

'I can see you've got a true English sense of priorities. No, as far as I know, the stupid animal wasn't hurt in any way. It came back scared and nervy with the saddle hanging round its tum, otherwise O.K.'

'I don't know why you call it *stupid*; personally I give it full marks for coming home on its own. I wonder if it fell or whether the boy just came off?'

'As I say, the animal wasn't hurt at all so presumably it didn't actually fall.'

'And the boy was lucky, too, not to have broken anything,' Berry said.

'I've been off half a dozen times without breaking anything,' Fen said. 'It depends how you fall.'

'I thought you were coming off at the water in the point-to-point,' Hooky said.

'So did I! Gaiety Girl knew a lot more about that jump than I did, I can assure you. By the way, have you heard the latest about the escaped convict?'

'Let me guess,' said Hooky. 'He's been invited by the Bishop of London to preach in St Paul's on the iniquities of the penal system, is that it?'

Berry, who was already on his way to the door, had turned back quickly. 'What is the latest about him?' he asked.

'Apparently the police think now that there may have been two motor-cycles involved.'

Berry stared at her.

'Two motor-cycles? What on earth makes anybody think that?' he asked finally.

'I don't know. I heard it on the radio just before coming out. The police have got this theory, but I can't see how it's going to help in any way.'

Berry went out.

'He doesn't think much of your theory,' Hooky said.

'It's not *my* theory; personally I don't give a damn if there were fifty motor-cycles involved. And I don't think much of *him*, anyway.'

'Captain Berry? What's wrong with him? He's all right.'

Fenella made a face. 'Maybe. I just don't like him, that's all. I wonder what he was a captain in? Is he married?'

'Yes, I have heard him speak about a wife.'

'I wonder what *she* thinks about him. Not much, I'll bet.'

Hooky didn't mind what Mrs Berry's view of her husband might be. Fenella's presence was acting like a tonic on him; Sheepsgate might have its worries and in time he would go back to them, but for the present they were forgotten.

Fenella teased him about his book.

'You authors are such unreliable people. At this moment you ought to be slaving away at the ending of chapter four.'

'Don't make indecent suggestions. At this moment I am quite content to be enjoying myself. Chapter four can wait. It's chapter five I'm looking forward to.'

'Why chapter five especially?'

'Enter the Princess.'

'Oh Hooky, tell me, what's she like?'

'Well, she's a good-looker; as a matter of fact, she's confoundedly pretty. Something of the gypsy about her. When I first saw her coming across the room towards me at Freddy Townsend's, that was what I thought—*gypsy*. There was something free and fine and bold about her. And she sits a horse tolerably well, a damned sight better than I ever shall, anyway; and I'm told she works in a flower shop in the Burlington Arcade, though how any flowers can be more attractive than she is I wouldn't know.'

'Hooky, what a nice thing to say.'

'But, then, I'm a nice person—or hadn't you noticed?'

'There must have been plenty of princesses, Hooky.'

'Plenty. And I'm not regretting one of them. It has all been fun. Good, clean, idiotic, romping, Bucks fizz-at-midnight fun with the minor characters in the cast, whilst I was waiting for the star to come on.'

'Hooky, Hooky, no pedestals. I'm not a star.'

'Are you not?'

'I never see her come into a room
But what I think, ah, not the fiddling's done
Now Life's brave footlights leap to stab the gloom
The curtain's up and see, the play's begun.'

Fenella caught the Archdeacon's eye and, because she was a little taken aback by what was being said, played for time by drawing him into things.

'Mr Hefferman is quoting poetry at me.'

'I'm very pleased to hear it, miss. A very proper thing to happen to a young lady like yourself, if I may say so.'

'You're a man after my own heart,' Hooky told him.

'Excuse me, Mr Hefferman, but when you were in here yesterday did I hear you mention your aunt?'

A shade passed over Hooky's face. 'Why bring that up?' he asked.

'Would that be the Honourable Mrs Theresa Page-Foley, sir?'

'My God, you make it sound like a declaration of war—which, of course, it only too often is. Don't tell me you know the old girl?'

'Mrs Page-Foley used to visit the Abbey occasionally, sir. His Grace always looked forward to her coming.'

'His Grace must have been a glutton for punishment.'

'A remarkable woman, Mr Hefferman. No longer as young as she once was, of course.'

'About a hundred and one.'

'And still hale and hearty, I expect?'

'I'm afraid so.'

'Wonderful.'

'Look, my dear old innkeeper, stop ghoulishly reminding me about the dark background of my life and concentrate on the pleasant present. I am about to invite Miss D'Aubiac to have lunch with me. Where would you recommend in Exdale as being suitable for such an occasion?'

'I'm afraid, Mr Hefferman, that Exdale has very little to offer in the way of gastronomic resources, there's nothing of which your Aunt would approve—'

'My Aunt doesn't approve of me, so leave her out of it.'

'—but if I might make a suggestion, sir, I could have a word with Mrs Jenkins and I am quite sure that she would be able to produce something, nothing elaborate, of course.'

'I hate elaboration,' Fenella chimed in, 'and I should simply love to have lunch here, Hooky. I can't think of anything nicer.'

'Me too,' Hooky said, and the Archdeacon beamed on them both.

They ate in the parlour behind the bar, a small room crowded with furniture and bric-à-brac of every sort, pride of place being given to a photograph of an eccentrically dressed old gentleman carrying a sort of shepherd's crook and surrounded by dogs, standing in front of a building rather like Wellington Barracks.

'His Grace,' the Archdeacon said. 'He disliked being photographed and I've seen him knock more than one camera to pieces with that stick of his.'

With many apologies for the inadequacy of what she was providing Mrs Jenkins produced a meal which the gastronomical gods themselves would hardly have found fault with—cold roast beef as tender as could be and cut very thin; two huge potatoes roasted in their jackets; an apple-pie of superlative quality and a noble piece of Double Gloucester to go with it.

'I've never enjoyed a meal more in my life,' Hooky declared.

'Super,' Fenella agreed. Wise and sophisticated person that she was she still retained certain childish traits of speech and manner which Hooky found very endearing. Her next remark alarmed him considerably.

'I'll be going back to London in a day or two, Hooky; but I'll ring you before I do.'

'You're going back to London?'

'I can't stay here for ever, can I? What about the poor Townsends? Besides I've a job to look after.'

'I shall come into the Burlington Arcade and buy a buttonhole every single day of my life.'

She laughed at him. 'Oh, Hooky, it's been such fun seeing you down here.'

'You don't have to go back yet surely?'

'But I do. Duty calls.'

'I can manage to be totally deaf when that tiresome old bag Duty starts bleating.'

'Nonsense, Hooky, you're a very self-disciplined and hardworking person, I can see that—'

'My God, you've got good eyesight.'

'—so settle down to your book; don't be too upset about the boy's disappearance; it wasn't your fault, and if I were you I'd keep a weather eye open on Captain Berry.'

'I think you're a bit prejudiced about Berry.'

'I wouldn't care to be his wife.'

The mad idea occurred to Hooky that it was then and there, that that was the precise moment, when he ought to say *Would you care to be my wife?* and he very nearly did so; but caution, not generally a Hooky-like trait, restrained him. Steady the Buffs, he told himself; hold your horses; play fair. Attractive as the idea is, you're probably not the marrying sort. In any case, she's about three thousand times too good for you, you old sinner; you've seen it all; you've been there; you've rubbed shoulders with it and a lot of the tarnish has come off on to you. True that no one else will light things up the way she does, but . . . but . . . but . . . .

Fenella had been watching him with some amusement.

'A penny,' she said.

'I'm tormented by indecision.'

'You undecided? Nonsense.' She laughed her gay young laughter. 'You're the most decidedly decided person I've ever met. It's one of the things I rather like about you.'

Hooky wondered what the others were.

THIRTEEN

LENNY LOOKED UP when the woman came into the loft. She was wearing slacks and a black jersey that fitted her thin body tightly; he ran his eyes over her.

'Christ, I'm getting bored up here,' he exclaimed by way of welcome. 'What's happening? Where is everybody?'

'Berry's gone into Exdale.'

Lenny smiled at her. 'Has he now? That husband of yours gone pub crawling again, has he? And you've come to tell me about it, eh?'

'He's gone to get some vodka.'

'Well, that will be nice for anyone who likes vodka, won't it? Personally I hate the stuff.'

'Big Boy likes it apparently.'

'Big Boy?'

'He was on the telephone last night and he said he might come down and take a look at things for himself.'

'As long as he gets me out of this bloody loft,' Lenny said. 'How long will Berry be away in Exdale?'

Betty lit a cigarette. 'I expect he'll stay in the pub a bit, long enough for a couple of drinks anyway.'

'I thought you didn't approve of smoking in a stable.'

'I don't—as a rule.'

'But you sometimes break rules, is that it?'

Betty answered that with a short sharp laugh and sheered away on a different conversational tack.

'It's that boy I'm scared of.'

'What's he up to now?'

'Well, it stands to sense he wants to be up and dressed and off back to Sheepsgate. He keeps asking why he can't go.'

'Where is he at the moment?'

'In his room. In bed, I hope. Anyway he can't do much; he hasn't got any clothes.'

'He's all right for the present then, isn't he? And your husband's away buying vodka, so what have we got to worry about?'

She looked at him levelly. 'I'm not worrying, Lenny.'

He shifted slightly to one side and patted the mattress he was squatting on.

'Makes a real comfortable old bit of a bed this does,' he said. 'Try it. . . .'

When they heard the sound of the Land Rover approaching the house Betty jumped up hurriedly. Lenny grinned in a satisfied male way at her. 'Tidy your hair a bit, for God's sake,' he advised. 'We've quite enough troubles on our plate as it is without any more complications.'

When Berry got out of the Land Rover Betty was coming away from the stable.

'Everything O.K.?' he asked.

'Yes, absolutely. Very much so. I've just been to have a word with Lenny. He's all right—a bit bored, of course. Did you get the vodka?'

Berry held out the two bottles he was carrying.

She nodded approval. 'Well done. Did you see anybody in the Huntsman?'

'That chap from Sheepsgate. Hefferman. Do you know what he told me?'

Betty raised her eyebrows.

'He's some sort of a private eye.'

The woman felt a slight stab of fear. 'A private eye? What's he doing down here?'

'Apparently he came down here with that kid we've got upstairs to keep an eye on him. Big Boy won't like the idea of a private eye poking about, I can tell you.'

'Hefferman hasn't been poking about up here.'

'Maybe not. Big Boy won't like it all the same. You haven't been up there all the time with Lenny in the loft, have you?'

'Don't be silly. I must just go occasionally to see how he's getting on, mustn't I? Did Hefferman say what they think has happened to the boy? Are they going on looking for him?'

'Doesn't matter if they are; they won't find him, will they?'

'Maybe not—but what are we going to do with him?'

'That's up to Big Boy; he'll tell us that when he comes.'

'*If* he comes; Lenny says he doesn't think he will.'

'What else did Lenny say?'

The woman laughed. 'Like I told you, he said he's bored and wishes to God he was out of it.'

'He's not the only one who wishes it. Well, if Big Boy doesn't come we'll open the vodka and have a go at it ourselves.'

But Big Boy did come. He arrived shortly after twelve sitting hunched up in the back of a huge black car driven by one of his personal guards. And he was in a very bad temper.

Berry and Betty went out into the drive to meet him.

'We ought to have been here an hour ago,' he complained as soon as he got out of the car. 'This bloody fool Jackson here said he knew the way. God, how he knew it! We've been going round in circles on these blasted roads for the last sixty minutes.'

'I think the map must be out of date,' the man at the wheel said nervously.

'You watch you don't get out of date,' Big Boy told him with venom. 'Out of date things and people are no good to me and just you remember it.'

Inside the house he began to be mollified by the effects of a large vodka. 'Where's Lenny?' he asked.

'In the hiding-place, in the loft.'

'Let's go and see him.'

In the stable his temper was roused again by the sight of the vertical wall-ladder. 'Am I expected to climb up that bloody thing?' he demanded.

'Lenny can come down.'

'No. I'll go up. Hell, I'm not a cripple or anything.'

Once up in the loft he nodded his head in approval of the hiding-place.

'You've done a good job here,' he told Berry. 'Comfortable up here, Lenny, aren't you?'

'Bored to tears, Chief.' Lenny was the only one of Big Boy's associates who used an individual name for him.

'Bored? Hell, what's that got to do with it? You'd be a damned sight more bored after twenty-five years inside, wouldn't you?'

'As you say, Chief.'

'Went all right, did it?'

'Like a dream. God Almighty, that stuff blew up right enough. I thought the end of the bloody world had come for a minute or two.'

'And the motor-cycle was O.K.?'

'Went like a bird. I'd like to get on it and shoot halfway across England away from these blasted moors.'

'Be your age, Lenny. Every police force in the country is looking out for a white solo Norton.'

'They found one in the car-park at Exeter station.'

'Yes, they did. Harry did his bit there all right; but the Law isn't entirely composed of nitwits and they are obviously on to the idea that that might have been a blind. Anyway, they are still looking out for a white Norton so we've got to be careful. Where is the machine now?'

'Four foot under water in the mud at the bottom of a pond at the end of the garden,' Berry said.

Big Boy considered and finally nodded approval.

'Probably as good a place as any. Nobody been round looking for anything?'

'Nobody's been here. They've been searching the moor for the boy; some of them still are searching probably.'

'Tell me about the boy.'

Berry gave an account of Simon's untimely arrival on the scene and Big Boy studied him with unblinking eyes as he did so.

'—and that's all there is to it.'

'All there is to it, eh?' Big Boy asked. 'You knew the timing. You knew the horse box with Lenny inside it would be here about half past four, but you couldn't take a walk round ten minutes beforehand to make quite certain nobody was about, could you?'

'But nobody ever does come here,' he explained. 'All day long we don't see anybody. Nobody comes.'

Berry moistened his lips slightly.

'Nobody comes!' Big Boy mimicked savagely. 'Nobody ever comes! But somebody *did* come, didn't they? And now we're landed with him. Where is the boy?'

'In bed. We're telling him his shoulder is worse than it really is.'

'I'll take a look at him in a few minutes.'

'And what about me, Chief?' Lenny asked.

'You'll be all right, Lenny boy. I'm getting things fixed up in Newcastle. There's a Norwegian ship goes across the North Sea from there. Regular sailing, all legitimate and above board, never been in trouble with the Law. We'll get you up to Newcastle from here and you'll go on board as a deckhand. With plenty of cash. Once you're on the other side it will be up to you.'

'Don't worry, Chief. Once I'm out of England they won't see me for dust. When do I go?'

'It won't be long now. It's got to be finally fixed up with the skipper of this Norwegian boat, and he isn't proving cheap, I can tell you. God, the prices people are asking for doing anything these days! But it won't be long. As soon as I've got it fixed I'll send word. And when you leave here,

Lenny, you go. Up to Newcastle. Non-stop. No farewell visits to that black bit of yours in Newington Road.'

'No fear, Chief.'

'I know what you are with women. He's a terror, believe me. Leave him alone with any woman for ten minutes and he's on top of her, aren't you, Lenny?'

'Belt up, Chief.'

'All right, all right. Just behave yourself, that's all. This little caper is costing money and I don't want it messed up now.'

'I'll be ready; believe me, I'll be ready.'

'Now, let's go and take a look at this goddamn boy.'

When they were down in the stable again Berry ventured on what he thought was a reasonably funny joke. 'You might pretend to be the doctor, come to have a look at his shoulder.'

Big Boy was not in the mood for jokes. Coming down the vertical wall-ladder had left him short of breath and temper.

'Is that meant to be a wisecrack?' he growled. 'I don't look like a doctor, and if I was ill I wouldn't have the sort of doctor who looked like me. Where is he?'

Simon was in bed reading when the door opened and Berry came into the bedroom accompanied by a short flabby man with fat white fingers. Simon didn't like the look of him. Berry stood in the doorway and the short flabby man asked questions. They were all about how he came to be there and his mishap on the horse and how badly he had hurt his shoulder. It didn't make much sense to Simon because all the questions had been asked before and everybody knew the answers to them. The fat man kept nodding all the time as Simon gave his answers. His eyes were fixed on the boy and Simon didn't like the uncanny way they seemed never to blink.

'And where do you live?' the man asked.

'In Stanmere Crescent, Hampstead.'

'Hampstead, eh? Father and mother live there, do they?'

'My father does. My mother's dead.'

'What did you say your name is—Loeson?'

'Yes, Simon Loeson.'

'Your father have anything to do with the show called Vandeem Press?'

'Yes, he owns it.'

Big Boy was an avid reader of the financial section of his daily paper and rumours about possible happenings involving the Vandeem Press and Market Enterprises had been bandied about pretty freely lately. He looked at the boy with fresh interest.

'And you were sent down here just for a holiday, is that it?'

'Yes.'

'And this man who came down with you—'

'Mr Hefferman?'

'Hefferman, is that his name?'

'Hooky Hefferman he's called.'

'Hooky, eh? What's he doing down here?'

'Well, he's with me. Sort of looking after me, I suppose.' The man nodded.

'Why can't I leave here?'

'Who says you can't leave here?'

'Captain Berry does.'

Big Boy turned to Berry in pretended surprise. 'You never told Simon he couldn't leave, did you?' he asked.

'Of course not. We've always told him when his shoulder is all right he can go at once, naturally.'

'That's what you've told them at Sheepsgate, is it?'

'Yes. Several times. On the telephone. They know all about it.'

Big Boy turned towards the bed again. 'There you are, then. Tomorrow or the next day maybe we'll send you over there in a car. Till then be a good boy. O.K.?'

Simon nodded.

'Got plenty to read and all that sort of thing?'

'Yes, I've plenty to read.'

'Nothing to worry about, then, is there?'

'No, nothing.'

When he was alone again Simon lay thinking. The fat man with the unblinking eyes had frightened him; the boy didn't believe for one instant that on the morrow or the day after there would be a car to take him back to Sheepsgate; he didn't believe anything of the sort would happen.

Downstairs in the living-room Berry asked, 'Vodka?'

'Yes. Plenty of it. And ice—I suppose you've got ice?'

'Yes, of course.'

Big Boy took the large drink without a word of thanks.

'A right mess you made having that boy on the scene,' he said.

Berry knew that he had to watch his step with the man, but he was beginning to tire of being found fault with.

'We can all overlook something,' he answered. 'After all, the bank job in Croydon High Street didn't go all that well, did it?'

For a moment it seemed as though Big Boy might fly into an ungovernable rage but in the end he contented himself with a short sharp laugh.

'No, it didn't. Quite right. That kid's father has got real money, you know.'

'Loeson? Rich is he?'

'Loaded. Tell him he can have his boy back if he gives us a hundred thousand and most likely we'd get it by return.'

'Kidnapping?'

'I've thought about it before now. And this might be a good chance to try it. But....' Big Boy shook his head, 'no sense in getting too much on our plate at once. What I'm interested in at the moment is seeing Lenny gets free—twenty-five years inside, can you imagine it?'

'And what happens to the boy? I want to get shot of him.'

'Don't worry, you'll be shot of him. The kid's dangerous. He saw Lenny and he saw the motor-bike. I'll have to
talk to a couple of men in the Smoke and then I'll send for
him.'

'Just as soon as you like,' Berry said. 'Another vodka?'

Big Boy held out his glass. 'You got a radio?' he asked,
'or haven't they got round to it yet in these God-forsaken
parts?'

'You want the one o'clock news?'

'Of course I want the one o'clock news. I want to hear
what the bastards are up to, don't I?'

Berry crossed the room and switched on the radio. The
weather forecast was in full spate and it seemed to annoy Big
Boy.

'Christ, how they do go on about the fornicating
weather,' he complained. 'Why the hell can't they get to the
news!'

The pips sounded, the news began...bloodshed in
Northern Ireland, railwaymen going on strike, the cost of
living up by six points....

'What a bloody country to live in,' Big Boy grumbled.

'...There is still no sign of the prisoner who made a sen-
sational escape from an outside working party on Dartmoor three days ago. A spokesman for Scotland Yard said
today that they are still not entirely satisfied that the white
Norton motor-cycle found abandoned in the car-park of
Exeter Station is the actual one concerned in the getaway
and police forces throughout the country have been alerted
to look out for a similar machine. Next the sports news....'

Big Boy made an impatient sign and Berry obediently
switched off the set.

'The Law can be alerted as much as it likes,' Big Boy said,
'but I don't think it's likely to come looking in the pond at
the end of your garden, do you?'

'No. I don't. I hope not, anyway.'

'Right. Well, I'll be getting back.'

'Won't you have some lunch?' Betty asked. 'There's nothing very special but I can manage a meal of sorts.'

'Lunch? I don't eat lunch. I don't eat anything till the evening. Everybody eats too much, anyway.'

'What about the man driving you? Wouldn't he like something?'

'I'm sure he would. But he won't get it. If I can wait till the evening, he can wait too. The bloody fool shouldn't have got lost bringing me here. If you two want to eat go ahead and eat. It won't worry me. Leave the bottle of vodka on the table here and I'll have a bit of a nap. I usually do about this time.'

Big Boy's 'bit of a nap' stretched far into the afternoon, and when he finally roused himself and, much to the relief of Berry and his wife, announced that he was ready to go his temper had evidently not improved.

'I don't propose to get lost on the way back,' he said. 'You've got a car, haven't you, Berry?'

'Yes, of course.'

'Right, you can give us a lead till we're on something like a main road again.'

'If I get you the other side of Exdale you'll be all right.'

'I don't give a damn what you call the place as long as you put us on a road where even the stupid idiot I've got driving me can't go wrong. Let's get going.'

'O.K. I'll lead the way in the Land Rover.'

Betty accompanied the two men out of the house. Big Boy didn't bother to say 'good-bye' to her; without a word he crammed himself into the back seat of his large black car whilst the driver nervously held the door open for him.

Berry was actually in the Land Rover when Betty called to him. 'Would you take the horse box instead and get it filled up in Exdale? It will save me going in this afternoon; here's the key.'

Big Boy lowered the window of his car and stuck his head half out. 'Make up your mind,' he roared. 'I don't care

which car you use as long as you show me the way out of
this God-forsaken place. Come on, let's get started.'

From the window of his bedroom Simon watched the
scene; he saw the fat man who had made him feel afraid get
into the back seat of a big saloon car, then Berry climbed up
into the Land Rover and almost at once came out again and
transferred into the horse box which was standing close by.
The boy guessed that this might be because Mrs Berry
wanted to use the Land Rover whilst her husband was away;
but it didn't look as though that was so because as soon as
the horse box, followed by this black saloon car, had gone
down the rough drive and disappeared out of sight Mrs
Berry turned and walked away quite slowly round the corner of the house. Simon thought that she must be going to
the stables to talk to the man who was hiding there. And Simon now had a very good idea who that man must be; the
boy had been listening at the top of the back stairs when the
pips went for one o'clock and the news had been read out.
He had heard about the escaped prisoner and the white
motor-cycle and he had suddenly begun to understand what
he had seen and what was happening to him.

In the bedroom he turned again to the window and looked
out at the Land Rover; he began to wonder how long Mrs
Berry would be in the stable.

The Land Rover was standing temptingly near to the
house, facing down the drive. Berry had been in such a
hurry to carry out Big Boy's wishes that the door of the
driving-seat was actually open.

As Simon stared out from the window his heart began to
race a little; he had never actually driven a Land Rover but
that didn't worry him much; with the sublime self-assurance
of fifteen the boy reckoned he knew all about driving any
sort of car; if by any chance the ignition key had been left
in the Land Rover Simon was quite sure that he could drive
the thing.

He was wearing pyjamas a great deal too big for him and an old untidy dressing-gown. He had on a pair of slippers but luckily these were pretty well the right size since he had large feet for his age and Berry's hands and feet were somewhat small. For a moment or two the boy thought about searching for his own clothes but he didn't know where to look and he realized that every minute was valuable. Mrs Berry was not likely to be in the stable long and if he was going to escape he must do it now.

He went out of the room, closing the door quietly behind him. At the end of the corridor he opened the door noiselessly and listened. He could hear nothing. Very cautiously he began to come down the stairs; halfway down one of them creaked loudly and his heart thumped; but there was nobody in the living-room and with urgency crowding in on him now he abandoned caution and took to speed.

He ran across the room, knocking a small table over in his hurry and so gained the front door, which was standing ajar. Only a few yards of gravel separated him from the Land Rover and when he clambered up into the driving-seat he had the sense not to slam the car door. A glance showed him what at that moment was the most blessed sight in the world—the ignition key left in position. He expected the gear lever to look a bit complicated but he had to chance his arm.

He started the engine and took a chance with the gear. The vehicle shot forward and Simon, frightened and exhilarated all at once, hung on to the wheel like grim death.

FOURTEEN

AFTER HIS MEMORABLE LUNCH in the Huntsman Hooky went straight back to Sheepsgate and rendered an account of his shopping expedition. Rachel declared herself delighted.

'You've done marvellously, Hooky. If I send Francis, bless his silly old heart, he always forgets something. If you were staying here for ever I should employ you as my permanent shopper. Did you go into the Huntsman?'

'I had lunch there.'

'Lunch? I didn't know Mr Jenkins did lunches.'

'I don't think he does really, but today he made an exception. It was something rather specially, really—'

'Special?'

'Well, for one thing, it turns out that Jenkins knows, or at any rate in the old days knew, my aunt.'

Rachel was disappointed; in her estimation there was nothing very special about an aunt and she said so.

'You don't know my Aunt Theresa.'

'She is something special?'

'She is more an elemental force of nature than a mere human being. Jenkins spoke of her with suitably bated breath.'

'Was anybody else in the Huntsman?'

'That chap Berry from Castlecroft looked in to buy a couple of bottles of vodka.'

'I suppose he had no news?'

'No, none. He was talking about the escaped prisoner most of the time.'

'I find I can't feel much interest in the escaped prisoner; it's Simon Loeson I'm worried about.'

'My God, aren't we all! Still, one thing Berry said about the prison escape did interest me rather....' Hooky's voice trailed away meditatively.

'And so you had lunch all by yourself?' Rachel prompted.

'Lunch? No, not exactly by myself. Fenella D'Aubiac came in—the girl I took to the point-to-point—and since she wanted lunch and I wanted lunch and good old Jenkins was willing to provide it, well, there you are; cold roast beef, baked potatoes, apple-pie and cheese.'

'Sounds lovely.'

'Food fit for the gods.'

Rachel laughed. 'I've never heard you sound so enthusiastic before about anything. Did Fenella D'Aubiac enjoy it too?'

'I think so. I hope so.'

Rachel studied him in silence for a few seconds and then asked gently, 'Is she very beautiful, Hooky?'

'I quoted poetry to her.'

'Hooky, how romantic! Do you know Francis writes me a Valentine every February.'

'Ah, but Francis is a good, well-behaved, sober citizen. I'm a reprehensible old reprobate.'

'Nonsense,' Rachel said briskly, 'any girl would be lucky to get you for her man. Hooky, I'm so interested in this and excited by it. Do tell me—are you in love with her?'

'I'm not only a reprehensible old reprobate,' Hooky answered, 'but I'm a crafty old cuss as well. I must have notice of that question. Meanwhile, can you help me in something?'

'Yes, of course. Anything.'

'You get the *Daily Mail* and the *Telegraph* every day, don't you?'

'Yes, why?'

'What happens to them?'

'All sorts of things. I always keep a stock of old papers; they come in handy for lots of purposes.'

'So the papers for the last three days won't have been burnt or got rid of yet?'

'Indeed they won't; they're neatly stacked in the back larder at this moment. Do you want to see them?'

Hooky did want to see them and he was busy reading through them when the sound of a car drawing up outside the farmhouse was followed immediately by Rachel's rushing in on him and exclaiming 'Charles Wilbury's just getting out of a car in the front drive and there's a man with him.'

'Loeson,' Hooky guessed at one, 'Simon's father. It's all Lombard Street to a china orange it's Loeson. And if it is he's pretty sure to be extremely unpleasant. Don't let him rile you, Rachel, let me handle him.'

Hooky's guess as to the identity of the visitor and his prediction as to the visitor's behaviour both turned out to be entirely correct. Loeson hurried from the car disregarding the man of law who, wearing a very worried look indeed, tagged on behind.

The front door was open and Loeson strode in, disregarding such trivial formalities as ringing the bell, or being invited to enter, or introductions of any sort. Hooky by this time was in the living-room and catching sight of him Loeson opened fire immediately.

'Where's my boy?'

'Unfortunately nobody knows, Mr Loeson.'

'*Unfortunately*—my God, this is good, the words you use. Unfortunately. What sort of unfortunately is this when a man's only son is lost?'

'Believe me, Mr Loeson—'

'Believe you? Why believe you? I do not believe you. A boy of fifteen, all you must do is to be with him. Tutor, guardian, companion, I don't care what you call it. Nothing else you have to do. So where is the boy now? Unfortunately nobody knows! For God's sake he must be somewhere—'

'Look, Mr Loeson, we all understand how you must be feeling and we all sympathize with—'

'Sympathize? Who wants sympathy? For ten pounds a day, seventy pounds a week, I don't want sympathy, I want you should do your job. Is the boy out on this moor somewhere?'

'Yes, he is; he must be.'

'*Must be!* If he must be why haven't you found him? Why aren't you looking for him? You are waiting here perhaps for him to come walking in and say what a nice time he has been having? Why aren't the police doing something?'

'The police have done a great deal and as a matter of fact are still on the lookout.'

'So now the police know all my business, eh?'

'The police know that a fifteen-year-old boy called Simon Loeson very foolishly disobeyed all orders about not riding Mrs Dobson's mare and as a result got himself lost on the moor. That's all they know, Mr Loeson; they know nothing about your business.'

'Business! I am astonished you should use the word. It must be a joke of some sort. An English joke perhaps which I am too ignorant to understand. How is business possible if everything I leave behind neatly arranged and taken care of is not done as soon as my back is turned? No sooner am I in South Africa on real business, business which is big, than on the telephone I am told what has happened here. In Johannesburg I am just starting negotiations; people are coming to see me; lunches, dinners, meetings, everything fixed; and I have to say no, I can't discuss your proposal, I shan't be there. I have to turn round and go straight back to England. So now is it morning, noon or night, I don't know. Flying and meals all the time and fasten your seat belts and the clock changing and no proper sleep. How is a man to do business like this? Is there any demand yet?'

'Any demand?'

'For ransom money. Or perhaps you haven't heard of ransom money. Perhaps you don't know that when somebody is kidnapped the next thing to his father is a note saying everybody knows you have a lot of money so pay up.'

'Simon hasn't been kidnapped, Mr Loeson.'

'No?'

'I'm sure of it.'

'You are sure of it. This is nice to be sure of anything. What I am sure of is that I said ten pounds a day for looking after my son and you don't look after him, so there is no ten pounds a day, there is not a single penny.'

That made Hooky laugh; he had already made up his mind not to accept any money for the job which had gone so disastrously wrong; now he realized that what he had to concentrate on was not losing his temper with the boy's father.

Rachel intervened to ask if Mr Loeson would like anything after his long motor-drive—a cup of coffee perhaps?

Loeson impatiently and angrily shook his head. 'Coffee? What good does a cup of coffee do when I am looking for my boy who should never have been allowed to get lost? Mr Wilbury says his cousin in the country takes in paying guests; he didn't tell me that you lose them as well.'

'Look, little man,' said Hooky, speaking slowly and with considerable restraint. 'You're Simon's father, so you are upset. O.K. Everyone is making allowances for that; but there's a limit. Blame me all you want to if it gives you any satisfaction, but don't start being offensive to Mrs Dobson. If you start off on that tack I shall be obliged to poke you in the nose good and hard.'

Loeson opened his mouth to say something in reply to this but a long hard look at Hooky made him think better of it.

'You understand that you are no longer in my employ?' he said.

'Good show. I am delighted to hear it.'

'You didn't do your job properly and I am entirely dissatisfied.'

'That's what the girl said to the soldier.'

In the end Charles Wilbury, who most of the time was hovering unhappily on the fringe of things, managed to get his rich client away before open warfare broke out.

'What an objectionable creature,' Rachel said when her unwelcome visitor had driven off. 'Of course, one feels sorry for him in the circumstances, but really! I think Charles ought to choose the people he acts for more carefully.'

'Charles chooses where the guineas are. He'll have a highly successful and distinguished career will our Charles.'

'I pity him if there are going to be many Mr Loesons in it.'

The telephone rang and Rachel went to deal with it.

'... Yes, he is.... Yes, of course you can.... Of course it's not any trouble. Hold on just one moment and I'll get him.'

'Somebody for you, Hooky,' she said into the room.

'For me?'

'A Miss Fenella D'Aubiac,' Rachel said, smiling at him.

'Hooky,' said the clear young voice, 'I've been thinking over our conversation in the pub this morning.'

'I've thought of practically nothing else since.'

'Ah, but listen. I mean I've been thinking about something Captain Berry said.'

'I thought you didn't like Captain Berry.'

'I don't.'

'Why dote on his words then—as a matter of fact, Berry let slip something which had been puzzling me quite a bit.'

'I wonder if it was the same thing that I spotted. What was yours?'

'Well, when we were talking about the escaped prisoner and the bomb in the hut business he said, "A bag of gellymix wouldn't be all that big." Remember?'

'Yes, I think I do; but what about it?'

'How did he know the bomb was made of gellymix? It was the first time I had ever seen the word used in connection with it. They take two papers here, the *Telegraph* and the *Mail*, and I've been looking carefully through their accounts of what happened. Columns about it, but not a word about gellymix. So, like I say, how did Berry know? Was that what you spotted?'

'No, I missed that. I supposed he might have guessed about it being gellymix?'

'Might have done, yes, I agree; but you know how a chance remark which you hardly notice at the time will lodge somewhere at the back of your mind and start to niggle at you an hour to two afterwards.'

'Like the bit about the horse did with me.'

'What bit about the horse?'

'Well, actually it was about the boy, but it followed on what I was saying about the horse. If you remember, I was asking you if the animal had fallen or got hurt in any way and you said it came home startled and a bit muddied but otherwise O.K.—'

'Yes, I remember that—'

'And then your chum Berry said, "The boy was lucky not to have broken anything." '

Hooky drew his breath in sharply.

'By God, so he did. So he did. He said the boy was lucky not to have broken anything. I was thinking about you riding over those desperate fences at the point-to-point and I didn't see the significance of it. If nobody has seen Simon since he disappeared how would Berry know whether the boy had broken anything or not?'

'The same thought occurred to me, Hooky; and that's why I'm ringing up. As tutor or companion to the boy, don't you think you ought to investigate it a little?'

'I ceased having anything to do with the boy officially about an hour ago. I was given the sack, I'm glad to say; which means that I can now act on my own.'

'And what are you going to do?'

'I always work better with an assistant—want a job?'

'Try to keep me out of it, that's all.'

'I think we'll pay a visit to Castlecroft and see what this Berry character looks like on his native heath.'

'Do you imagine we shall actually find the boy there, Hooky?'

'The dear Lord knows what we shall find. Very likely a mare's nest; possibly a crock of gold at the foot of the rainbow; could even be a rough house. Are you on?'

'When do we start?'

'I'll get into the Jag straight away so I ought to be with you in, what, twenty minutes?'

'I'll be ready.'

Hooky did the journey in a shade under twenty minutes, apologizing all the time to his aged chariot for pushing her so hard over the atrocious roads. When he drove up to Fenton Park the slim, trim figure in slacks and a polo-necked jersey was standing on the terrace ready for him. A lot of girls would have kept him waiting—but not this one, he thought, not this one.

He drew the Jag to a halt and opened the door on the passenger side; the young shapely figure settled down in the seat, close to him and he was keenly and deliciously aware of her femininity.

'All right?' he queried.

'Absolutely.'

'Sure you want to come?'

'Don't be silly, Hooky.'

'Like I said, it will probably end up being a mare's nest.'

'I've never seen a mare's nest so I shall be interested.'

'I'm afraid it won't be a very comfortable ride. These boys down here don't seem to have done much about their roads since the Romans built one or two.'

'There's no hurry. We've plenty to talk about. Since we spoke on the phone I've been looking through the papers here for the past few days.'

'What do they take?'

'*The Times*, the *Guardian* and the *Express*; and the word gellymix doesn't occur in any of them. They all simply talk about "a bomb". What *is* gellymix, by the way? I've become quite interested in the stuff now.'

'It's based on gelignite, of course, and it looks more like putty than anything else. ICI make it amongst others and it's used for blasting in quarries and tunnelling and so on; and of course, in these civilized and enlightened days, for blowing shops and buses and women and children to pieces all in the sacred causes of religion and freedom.'

'Will people ever be civilized and enlightened, Hooky?'

'Extremely unlikely. Which is just as well in a way, because if they ever do private eyes will go out of business.'

'It was clever of you to spot Berry's slip about the gellymix.'

'Come off it, Fen. You're the clever one. Berry could have guessed that gellymix would be used for the bomb; that's possible; but it *isn't* possible that he would know whether Simon had broken anything or not unless he has seen the boy since the accident.'

'But if they are hiding the boy at Castlecroft—*why*?'

'God knows. The more I think about it the less sense it makes. Simon's father has got this kidnapping idea firmly fixed in his head, of course—'

'You're not backing that horse?'

'How can you? Like I say, it doesn't make sense. The Berrys were established down here months ago and neither they nor anybody else could have had any idea that Simon was going to be sent to Sheepsgate. They simply had no connection with the boy; and now we are looking at the possibility that they find him lying on the moor, or wandering about lost, and they take him in, hide him, and swear they know nothing about it all.'

'It just doesn't add up,' Fenella said.

'Which is why I like it. I like things that don't add up—

to think that two and two make four
and neither five nor three
the heart of man has long been sore
and long 'tis like to be.'

'You're a great man for quoting poetry, Hooky.'
'Sometimes I get inspired.'

The road they were on ran down a long incline to a hollow with a patch of woodland on either side; the surface was better than they had been enduring for some time and Hooky pressed on the accelerator slightly. There was the promise of adventure in the air and he had the most attractive girl he had ever known by his side; he was on the point of bursting into song when he reached the bottom of the long slope and the other car, masked until that moment by the copse of pine trees, hit him.

FIFTEEN

HOOKY WAS A GOOD DRIVER and on the whole he had been a lucky one so that his ears had very seldom been assailed by the sickening sound of metalwork grinding into metalwork.

The realization that it was happening to his beloved Jag appalled him. The noise of the crash died away and was succeeded by an unnatural silence. After a couple of seconds Hooky, who was feeling considerably shaken, found his voice.

'Are you all right, Fen?'

Fenella gave a nervous little laugh.

'Yes. I—I think so. I seem to be all in one piece still. Are you hurt, Hooky?'

'No. Perfectly O.K. Sure you're all right? Nothing broken?'

The worst shock of the accident was already beginning to wear off a little.

'No. Everything in working order. A bit shaken up. What a frightful bang.'

'I hadn't the vaguest idea there was a side road there,' Hooky said. 'God, did you see the way that bloody lunatic came batting out of it?'

On more considered reflection Fenella might have come to the conclusion that Hooky himself had been batting along at no mean speed, but the confusion and uncertainty of the accident were still on her and all she said was 'Thank goodness we're both all right, Hooky. I wonder what's happened to the other driver?'

With some difficulty Hooky extricated himself from his battered car and took stock of the situation. The force of the impact had swung the Jag right across the road, blocking it; the other vehicle was half on the road, half in the shallow ditch at the side. It was a Land Rover and Hooky was annoyed to observe that it didn't appear to have suffered anything like as badly as his Jag.

As he approached it he was assembling in his mind as choice and original a collection of oaths as he had ever used. When he wrenched open the door of the Land Rover an indignant voice demanded, 'Why didn't you sound your horn?'

Hooky, not often completely non-plussed, was now for a moment speechless. It was not so much the unreasonableness of the query that staggered him as the fact that he found himself confronted by Simon Loeson. He watched in almost unbelieving astonishment as the boy climbed out from the Land Rover with some difficulty and stood in the road by the side of it.

Hooky noticed, but in the first moment of bewilderment hardly realized the fact, that the boy was wearing pyjamas and a dressing-gown.

'Where in the name of all hell have you sprung from?' Hooky demanded.

'I've escaped.'

'Escaped? Where from?'

'Those people who kept telephoning you to say they hadn't seen me; I was there all the time.'

'You mean the Berrys at Castlecroft?'

'This is their Land Rover. I told you I could drive. I'd have been O.K. if you hadn't run into me.'

Hooky blinked; he could see he was going to need a great deal of self-restraint. He forced himself to speak calmly.

'Are you all right, Simon?' he asked. 'Are you hurt in any way?'

'My shoulder still hurts a bit. I did it when I fell off that stupid horse.'

Hooky shut his eyes and prayed silently for strength.

'We'll talk about that later,' he said. 'By God, we'll talk about that later. What are you dressed like that for?'

'I'm not dressed.'

'God Almighty, boy, that's what I mean.'

'I had to be in bed the first day because of my shoulder and then they kept me there.'

'Why?'

'They wouldn't let me have my clothes back.'

'Simon—*why*?'

'I suppose it was because I saw the man come out of the horse box.'

'What man?'

'And I saw the motor-cycle, the white Norton, as well.'

The whole affair seemed to Hooky to be soaring away into the realms of nightmare.

'You saw a man and a white Norton motor-cycle?' he asked.

'I just said so. Then I heard something about it on the radio news, so I think he must be the escaped prisoner, don't you?'

'And where is this man now?'

'I think he must be the one in the stable at Castlecroft.'

It began to dawn on Hooky that things after all were capable of making sense, that there might be a pattern in the jigsaw after all. His thoughts were interrupted by Simon exclaiming with unconcealed relish, 'Gosh, you've made a mess of your Jag all right, haven't you?'

A number of possible replies rose to Hooky's lips, but Fenella was there and he suppressed them.

'Let's get this quite clear...' he began quietly.

'It's all perfectly clear to me,' Simon answered him.

'That's because you are a heaven-born bloody genius,' Hooky said. 'We all know that, of course. You're so damned clever that you did what everybody had told you fifty times not to do. You took Mrs Dobson's horse out and naturally enough came to grief on it.'

'The saddle slipped.'

'The saddle slipped because you hadn't the foggiest clue how to do the girth up. What I want to know is where and when did you see this man you are talking about and the white motor-cycle?'

'At Castlecroft. I didn't know it was Castlecroft then, of course. I didn't know where I was. I was lost. And I was a bit scared as well. I had been in a bog.'

'And you came across Castlecroft by accident?'

'Yes. I was wandering about, trying to find my way back to Sheepsgate, then suddenly there was this house and some people there so of course I went up to them.'

'There's a van or something coming down the hill,' Fenella said.

What was coming down the hill was a horse box. Captain Berry had thankfully got rid of Big Boy at last and was on his way back to Castlecroft. Seeing what was obviously the aftermath of a crash ahead of him he brought the horse box to a halt; in fact he had no choice in the matter for one of the cars involved was slewed across the narrow road and there wasn't room to get by. It wasn't until Berry got out and went nearer on foot that he suddenly began to realize a whole lot of things—most of them unpalatable.

A smile began to spread over Hooky's face as he recognized who it was joining the party.

'Well, well, well,' he said. 'Talk of the devil. We were just speaking about you.'

By this time Berry had weighed up the situation pretty accurately. Once again he made a quick assessment of how far the Jaguar was straddled across the road and he was forced to come to the same conclusion—there just wasn't room to drive round it. The all-important thing was to get back to Castlecroft somehow and warn Lenny. If Lenny isn't warned, he thought, God knows what that bastard Big Boy will say—or do.

He had bluffed himself out of awkward situations before and there was just a chance that he might do so again.

When he spoke it was quite jauntily.

'You seem to have had a bit of a mix-up. What's happened?'

'Simon and I ran into one another accidentally,' Hooky said. 'By the way, you know Simon, don't you?'

'Simon?'

The only feasible plan was already beginning to form in Berry's head: the horse box, he recognized, would have to be abandoned, there wasn't room to get it past the stranded Jag and it was too big and cumbersome to be reversed on the unfenced moorland road without grave risk of getting bogged in the soft turf at the side; but the Land Rover—which presumably the boy must have made a getaway in—looked all right, and that would reverse without danger. If he could keep talk, however nonsensical, going for a few minutes and work his way towards the vehicle it might be possible to make a dash for it.

'Simon?' he repeated.

'Simon Loeson,' Hooky said. 'This boy here, wearing what I assume must be a pair of your pyjamas and I can't say I think much of your taste in slumberwear.'

Berry looked at Simon with a splendidly simulated stare of surprise.

'I've never seen the boy before in my life,' he said. Hooky laughed; he could see that this customer would have to be dealt with and dealt with in a pretty elementary way. It was a considerable time since Hooky had been mixed up in any sort of rough house and he feared that he might be somewhat out of practice; but, given all the circumstances, he didn't see any practical alternative.

'So you've never seen Simon before?' he asked.

'Never. Is this the boy who got lost?'

'And some kind people took him in and put him in bed and kept him there. Nice of them, wasn't it?'

'So now everything's all right? Well, that's fine, then, isn't it?'

Whilst he was talking Berry was unobtrusively edging his way towards the Land Rover. Hooky, becoming aware of what was happening, realized the danger—let this joker make a sudden dash and get inside the driving-seat of the Land Rover, he thought, and it might be very difficult to stop him getting clean away; he thought it was time to apply the closure.

'And *now* who's joining us?' he asked jerking his head up and looking over Berry's shoulder.

It was the oldest trick in the book, but unfortunately for Captain Berry he hadn't been reading the book lately. He fell for it hook, line and sinker. The last thing he wanted was that anybody else should be joining them; anybody else on the scene would complicate matters; he turned his head swiftly to see who it was.

As Berry turned his head, thinking of nothing for the moment but of who the newcomer on the scene might be, Hooky hit him. It was a good clean blow, straight to the point of the chin, with all the weight of the powerful pair of shoulders behind it; it would have knocked anybody out, and the unsuspecting Berry went down like a sack of potatoes.

Hooky thought he had probably broken a couple of knuckles, but he couldn't bother about that for the moment. A knockout didn't last for ever and he had to act quickly.

'There's some cord in the boot of the Jag,' he told Simon. 'Get it out and let's get this customer tied up, then we can decide what to do.'

As the coil of thin cord was being unwound Simon said, 'I don't know if you know anything about knots. I'm quite good at them. I—'

'Stop talking,' Hooky growled at him, 'and get on with it.'

Berry was already beginning to stir, consciousness forcing its way back uneasily into a still-muddled brain; but by now his ankles were tied together and so were his wrists and Hooky could suck his painful knuckles at his leisure.

'Is your hand hurt?' Fenella asked.

'Broken in two, I should think, by the feel of it. I hit him hard.'

'You certainly did, Hooky, you certainly did.'

'I'm getting too old for this sort of lark. Still, what else could I do?'

'Nothing. You couldn't do anything else, Hooky. You were marvellous.'

Hooky grinned at her. He reckoned it was worth a busted knuckle or two to hear Fenella say that.

'And what now?' she asked.

'I don't suppose there's a telephone within miles in this God-forsaken part of the world,' Hooky said, 'but a telephone is what we want.'

'Actually there's one a few hundred yards up the road. An AA box,' Simon corrected him. 'I came by it just before you crashed into me.'

With considerable self-restraint Hooky refrained from commenting on Simon's assessment of the incident and despatched Fenella to the AA box to make a 999 call to the police.

'Tell 'em we've got three vehicles here and a villain tied up and it's all a bit of a shambles,' Hooky instructed her.

Whilst she was away he propped Berry into a sitting position against the Jag and lit a cigarette for him.

'Sorry I had to sock you,' he said, 'but you really over-played your hand a bit with Simon, didn't you?'

'You'll get six months for assaulting me.'

'That's always possible,' Hooky admitted. 'The Law's a cock-eyed affair. You find out it isn't all Z cars and Dixon of Dock Green stuff when you come to look into it.'

'And the boy will go to Borstal for stealing my Land Rover.'

'That might not be such a bad idea,' Hooky agreed, 'but of course first of all you will have to explain how he came to be at Castlecroft and yet you knew nothing about his being there; by the way, what happened to the Norton motor-cycle?'

'I haven't any idea what you are talking about.'

'A very wise attitude, if I may say so. Defensive batting. Say nothing and leave the Law to prise it out of you, if they can—which, incidentally, they can't always do.'

'I never quite swallowed your tale about being an author.'

'It's a bit improbable, I agree; but the funny thing is it's true. I have been slogging away at a book down here.'

'And doing private-eye work looking after the boy. What's so special about him—his rich father?'

'Now, as you've never seen Simon before I wonder how you know he's got a rich father? That's the sort of slip you don't want to make when the Law starts asking questions.'

'Get stuffed,' said Captain Berry sourly.

Fenella came back from her expedition to the AA telephone box not many minutes before the arrival of two police cars on the scene. A sergeant and a constable were in the first one, a solitary constable in the second. The sergeant was a thin, dark, hard-bitten, disbelieving man who in the course of twenty-six years' service in the force had come to the conclusion that not only were all men liars but all women too, only more so.

He got out and surveyed the scene.

He saw three vehicles, two of which had obviously been in an accident; a man sitting propped up against one of the cars, his wrists and ankles tied; a youth wearing what looked like a dressing-gown (a hippy? he wondered); a chunky-looking customer whose right hand was bleeding slightly; and a good-looking young woman.

He was glad to see the good-looking young woman there. She confirmed his theory that when you have trouble you nearly always find a woman; and the better looking she is the worse trouble you've got.

'And who was it telephoned?' Sergeant East asked.

'I did.'

The sergeant took a long look at Fenella.

'Did you?' he said at last. 'So what's the trouble? Why is this man tied up?'

'I'm tied up,' Berry said in his best pseudo-military voice, 'because I have been assaulted. My car has been stolen and I have been assaulted. Knocked out and tied up.'

Sergeant East nodded. Whether he accepted it all as gospel truth or didn't believe a single word it was quite impossible to say.

'Anybody here claim to have done all that?' he asked.

Feeling rather like a small boy at the back of class owning up to a misdemeanour Hooky said, 'I knocked him out, yes.'

The sergeant's eyes travelled once more to Hooky's damaged knuckles.

'Did you, now?' He spoke to one of his constables. 'Loader, get this man untied, but keep an eye on him; keep an eye on everybody.' He waited until Berry's wrists and ankles were free and then addressed the class again.

'Now, listen, you lot. I don't know what this is all about so I shall have to start and ask a few questions, and I think I'll begin with you,' he pointed to Hooky.

'You couldn't have made a better choice,' Hooky answered him. 'Get your little book out, give your pencil a good lick and listen. You must know that there's been a fifteen-year-old boy missing from Captain Dobson's place at Sheepsgate for the past three days and you will certainly be aware that a prisoner got away from Dartmoor on a Norton motor-cycle—well, the missing boy and the escaped prisoner and the motor-cycle all come into this—'

'Do they?' Sergeant East said in utterly non-committal tones. 'Well, that's interesting; tell me how.'

Hooky told him how, succinctly and picturesquely; whilst listening to it all the expression on the Sergeant's dark, lean face altered not one little bit.

He next turned to Simon.

'And you say you were kept at Castlecroft against your will?'

'Of course I was.'

'Locked in, were you?'

'No, I wasn't actually locked in. If I had been locked in I couldn't have got out, could I? I was in bed.'

'Why were you in bed?'

'Because I hurt my shoulder when I fell off the horse.'

'So the people at Castlecroft took you in and looked after you, is that right?'

'In a way. Then when I was better they kept telling me I wasn't better. So I ran away. I escaped.'

'How did you manage that?'

'I took Captain Berry's Land Rover and everything would have been all right if Mr Hefferman hadn't run into me here, at this corner.'

'Have you got a driving licence?'

'Of course I haven't got a driving licence. I'm only fifteen. That isn't old enough to get a driving licence. Surely you know that?'

Sergeant East blinked a little but he made no comment.

'Tell me about the man and the motor-cycle you saw coming out of the horse box,' he said.

Simon told him. The Sergeant listened in silence and then turned his attention to the man still sitting on the ground, his back resting against the Jag but now with his hands and feet free.

Captain Berry chose to give his full name—'Captain Edward Baillie-Wilson'—and he loudly and vehemently disclaimed all knowledge of everything that had been alleged.

'The whole thing is a tissue of lies,' he exclaimed. 'I've never seen this boy before. Whilst I was away from the house he obviously tried to steal my Land Rover and now he finds himself involved in a crash he dreams up all this cock-and-bull story. The Land Rover doesn't seem to be damaged and if it's all right I'll be content to forget the whole affair. It was a boyish escapade and the whole thing isn't worth powder and shot.'

'You'll overlook being assaulted?'

'Tempers flared up like they do at times; but no real harm done.'

'You say you've never seen this boy before?'

'He is nothing to do with me; how could I have seen him?'

'May I suggest something?' Fenella said putting in her oar for the first time.

Sergeant East cocked an eye at her. Every other member of the party was already mentally booked for a crime or misdemeanour of one sort or another: assault and battery; driving without a licence; detaining someone against his will. He wondered what he was going to be able to allege against the good-looking girl. The Sergeant was not a Kipling fan and so was ignorant of the quip about the female of the species being more deadly than the male; had he known the quotation he would almost certainly have approved of it; appearances seemed to tell him that the girl was a well-bred, well-balanced young lady; but the Sergeant was a sceptical man and had long since ceased to trust appearances.

He didn't reply directly to Fenella's query, but his general manner indicated that he would be interested in anything she had to say, without, of course, committing himself to believing a word of it.

What Fenella said was unexpected.

'Simon, would you come here a moment?'

Surprised the boy crossed over to her.

'Bend your head forward a little, would you?' Simon did as she asked and Fenella fumbled at the nape of his neck. What she discovered there seemed to please her.

'Sergeant, would you take a look at this?' she invited.

'This', when Sergeant East walked across and took a look at it, turned out to be a small linen tab neatly sewn into the neckband of the pyjama jacket and carrying the woven initials 'E.B-W.'

Sergeant East studied it without comment; but he was thinking vigorously: pretty smart, that; pretty smart. I wonder if she knew it was there, or if it was just guess-work? Either way it's smart.

He remembered that the name Edward Baillie-Wilson was already written down in his notebook and he thought it was going to be very interesting listening to E.B-W.'s explana-tion of how a boy he had never seen before in his life came to be wearing a pair of his pyjamas.

The Sergeant already strongly suspected that a good deal was going on which he hadn't yet got hold of; the sight of the name tab confirmed him in this view.

He raised his voice. 'All right, then, we can't settle this lot here, that's obvious. Loader, you'll take Captain Baillie-Wilson back to the station in the second car—'

'I'm not going to the police station,' Berry objected.

'I'm afraid you are, sir.'

'I demand to be allowed to go on my way, to Castlecroft, where I'm living.'

'You'll be quite free to do that later, sir. For the present Police Constable Loader will run you down to the station and you can make a statement there.'

'I don't wish to make any statement.'

'Nobody can force you to make a statement, but you will be given the opportunity of doing so.'

'What about my Land Rover and the horse box?'

'I shall leave a constable on the scene here in charge of these three vehicles.'

'And what are you going to do?'

'That's my business. I'll attend to that.'

'What if I refuse to be taken to the station?'

'I wouldn't advise you to do that. And when you're down there you can take out a summons against this man for as-saulting you. Before you go, Loader, get on your two-way to the station and tell them there is reason to think that the escaped prisoner may be at a house called Castlecroft. They had better send an extra car up there to meet me and warn the road blocks again until we find out what's what.'

When Police Constable Loader had finally driven off taking Captain Berry with him the Sergeant turned to Hooky.

'I'm going to ask you and this young lady and the boy to come with me to Castlecroft,' he said. 'Have you any objection?'

'None whatever,' Hooky told him. 'In fact, I should have felt very much hurt if you had left me out of things.'

'I haven't the slightest intention of doing that,' Sergeant East assured him dryly. 'Would you get in the car, please?'

IN HIS HIDING-PLACE at the end of the Castlecroft loft Lenny was feeling better for Big Boy's visit. In one way, of course, it had been unsettling. Big Boy smelt of the Smoke; of the outside world that Lenny knew and understood and longed for; of streets and pubs and restaurants and race courses; of noise and movement and women whenever you wanted them . . . and then Newcastle—what went on up in Newcastle? Much the same as anywhere else, Lenny supposed, only he wouldn't know his way around. Still, it would be Newcastle only for a day or two, maybe not even so long, and after Newcastle Norway. How the hell he was going to get on in Norway Lenny (a true Cockney if ever there was one) couldn't imagine; still, Big Boy had said there would be plenty of cash and, foreign parts or not, Norway was going to be Paradise compared to twenty-five years in Dartmoor.

He glanced at the woman sitting on a hay-bale close by and smoking.

'You've been breaking rules again,' he teased her.

'I shall be glad when you've gone, Lenny.'

'That's a nice thing to say. Why?'

'You're. . . .' Betty hesitated then made a grimace which was half a smile, half an expression of disgust. 'You're *disturbing*.'

'Don't tell me you haven't enjoyed it. You're good at it, too.'

The woman flicked the ash off her cigarette and asked, 'What will you do in Norway?'

'Look for somebody like you.'

'You'll have forgotten all about me in a month.'

Lenny laughed. 'Very likely. It doesn't pay to remember things. I wonder how soon Big Boy can get it fixed up?'

A sound alerted the woman and she lifted her head quickly.

'That's the Land Rover,' she said.

'I thought you said he had taken the horse box.'

'So he did. But that wasn't the horse box and anyway he wouldn't be back yet.'

'Go and take a dekko round, for God's sake.'

In a few minutes she was back in the loft again, white-faced.

'What's up?'

'The boy's gone.'

'*Gone?* How the hell could he go? He didn't have any clothes, you told me.'

'He must have gone in his pyjamas and he's taken the Land Rover.'

'You never said he could drive.'

'Damn it, Lenny, I didn't have the vaguest idea he could drive. I never thought of him in connection with the car. He's only fourteen or fifteen.'

They stared at one another.

'So what's the next move?' Lenny asked at length.

'He'll go to Sheepsgate and tell the people there what's happened.'

Lenny drew a deep breath and expelled it slowly. 'By God, you and your man between you have cocked up this lot all right. Big Boy will have something to say to this, I can tell you.'

'What about the motor-cycle?'

Lenny stared at her, his imagination caught by the idea for a moment. He could feel the prison walls closing in on him again and it was a terrible sensation. He remembered the first glorious twenty minutes of his escape when freedom and movement had made him feel drunk.

'It's under water somewhere, didn't you say?'

'Yes, in the pond at the end of the garden. I suppose we could get it out.'

'It'll take the best part of a day to dry it out and get it in working order, even if we are able to work on it, which we won't be with the Law tramping about all over the place.'

'You think they'll come here?'

'Be your age, for God's sake. Of course the bastards will come.' He shook his head. The motor-cycle idea was desperately appealing but he knew it wouldn't work. Even if the machine could be put into running order after having been in mud and water for three days there would be no future in it. Every policeman and every garage in the south of England would be looking out for a white Norton. T.V. would see to that.

'That bloody television,' he said aloud bitterly.

The woman caught the drift of his thoughts and nodded in sympathy.

'So what will you do?' she asked.

He had made up his mind by now. 'Stay here. The boy doesn't know about this actual hiding-place and they may miss it. When they come your spiel is that I was lying up in the stable for a couple of days and now I'm gone again. On foot, across the moor. You've no idea where. Or else, if you want, you can say I never came here and the boy's making it all up. Maybe that's better. Of course, they'll turn your house upside down looking for me but you can give me some water and some grub—cheese, bread, biscuits, anything—and I can stick it out for two or three days easily. It'll be a lot better than solitary inside, I can tell you. And when the bastards have gone after a couple of days of looking and finding nothing we can think again. Maybe Big Boy will come up with something.'

'Berry will be back any minute now. Perhaps he'll think of something.'

'The only thing to think of is what I've just told you. If I go charging around the countryside on that Norton they'll get me. Certain. I'll be able to lie up here for three days, a week even, until the heat is off and then do something about it. Put Berry in the picture as soon as he gets back so that he says the same thing as you and start getting that grub and water ready.'

The woman was busy in the kitchen when she heard the car. She was standing at the table getting the supply of food ready for Lenny and she stopped what she was doing and jerked her head up to listen. She heard the sound of a car engine, but it wasn't familiar. It wasn't either the horse box or the Land Rover. She opened the back door of the kitchen and went outside, her heart hammering a little. To her dismay she saw the blue and white of a police car. Standing there looking at it she felt sick.

Simon and three other people got out of the car: a thin, tall police sergeant; a square-shouldered tough-looking man whose right hand had a handkerchief wrapped round it; and a girl. She had never seen any of them before. *Where in God's name is Berry,* she wondered.

The Sergeant approached her with the other two a few paces in the rear.

'Mrs Baillie-Wilson?' he asked.

She nodded, feeling obscurely that a mere nod somehow committed her less than a verbal 'yes'.

Sergeant East had for so long been accustomed to seeing that mythical entity called the Truth so neglected, despised, abjured and distorted that he himself had not the least hesitation in straining it a little now.

'I'm sorry to tell you that your husband has been involved in a slight accident,' he said.

'Is he hurt?'

'No. He isn't hurt in any way.'

'Where is my husband, then?'

'He's at the station, helping us with some enquiries.'

The woman didn't like the phrase. Sergeant East hadn't intended that she should like it; he thought she looked tough and competent; very well able to take care of herself; not an easy nut to crack by any means. Shake her a bit, he thought.

'What enquiries?' she asked slowly, her eyes fencing with his.

'We've been looking for a boy called Simon Loeson.'

'Simon Loeson?'

The Sergeant didn't help her by repeating the name; he waited in silence for her to continue, staring at her.

'This boy here,' the sergeant continued at length indicating Simon.

'We say he had an accident riding and you looked after him here. Put him in bed and so on?'

Betty moistened her lips. She couldn't guess how much they knew; she couldn't make up her mind whether it was worth while trying to bluff things out; she didn't know what to do. She felt sick with fright.

'Is that right, Mrs Baillie-Wilson?'

'Well, as the boy was injured anyone would help him, naturally, wouldn't they?'

'But I understand that you told Major and Mrs Dobson on the telephone that you hadn't seen anything of the boy.'

'Who told you that?'

'It doesn't matter who told me that. Is it true?'

'Yes, perfectly true.'

The first grip of fear was slackening a little. He's asking questions, she thought, but he can't know everything; he may not know much; if I keep my head and am careful not to give anything away something might yet be saved.

'Why should you have said that?' the Sergeant asked.

'Because Simon asked us to. He came in here out of the blue with an injured shoulder so naturally we looked after it for him which meant putting him to bed for a couple of days. He wasn't very coherent at first; we gave him a sedative that first evening and next day when he was better and we asked him questions about where he came from and so on. He told us he was very unhappy at Sheepsgate and he begged us not to make him go back there.'

'He asked you not to tell Major and Mrs Dobson where he was?'

'That's exactly what I am explaining to you.'

'And you thought that was the proper thing to do?'

'I thought the boy was unhappy at Sheepsgate and I didn't see why he should go back there if he didn't want to. After all, it isn't his home.'

Sergeant East consulted his notebook for a few seconds before continuing.

'I expect you know that a prisoner by name Lenny Dawson escaped from a working party on Dartmoor three days ago.'

'I saw something about it on T.V.'

'This man got away on a white motor-cycle, a Norton.'

'I remember hearing that too.'

'Simon Loeson says that he saw a man and a white Norton cycle being taken out of a horse box here at Castlecroft.'

The woman managed to laugh almost convincingly.

'I'm afraid you are having your leg pulled, Sergeant,' she said. 'Simon heard all about the escaped prisoner on the radio like the rest of us and lying in bed with his strained shoulder he must have made up this extraordinary story. You don't really believe it, do you? What on earth should we be doing here at Castlecroft with an escaped prisoner and his motor-bike from Dartmoor. I can assure you of one thing, if Captain Baillie-Wilson ever came across an escaped convict he would be the first person to hand him over to the police.'

'So you've seen nothing of this man Dawson and his motor-cycle?'

'Of course not. Why the word of a hysterical schoolboy whom we were trying to befriend should be believed before ours I really can't imagine.'

'I'm not saying what I believe or don't believe; but we have to make enquiries, Mrs Baillie-Wilson, don't we?'

The woman shrugged her shoulders.

'So you won't mind if I have a look round?'

'Not in the slightest. If you find an escaped prisoner anyway or a—what sort of motor-cycle did you say it was? A white Norton? You'll let me know, won't you? I should be interested.'

'I should like to start with the stables,' the Sergeant said.

'Start where you like. But, please, none of you smoke in the stable. I don't like it.'

Hooky, following slightly in the rear, obediently threw his cigarette to the ground and trod on it. He couldn't help feeling a certain admiration for Mrs Baillie-Wilson; he thought Sergeant East had come up against a tricky one here.

Rufus turned round in his horse box to have a look at his visitors; Fenella spoke a word to him and fondled his muzzle for a friendly moment.

The stable was not a big place and the Sergeant walked round it slowly and methodically.

'And where does that go to?' he asked when he reached the vertical wall-ladder.

'Up into the loft; and the escaped convict rode straight up it on that white motor-cycle of his and disappeared from sight. It was as good as the Indian rope-trick. Do go up and have a word with him there, please.'

Sergeant East nodded. Like most policemen he had acquired over the years a special protective coating against sarcasm so that he hardly noticed it. 'I think I will,' he said. 'Are you coming up with me, Mrs Baillie-Wilson?'

'Why should I bother?' Betty answered. 'There's nothing to see.'

It cost her an effort not to go into the loft with the Sergeant but instinct told her that it would be more convincing if she refused. She knew that the false wall at the far end was safely in position with the odds and ends of binder twine and general junk lying against it; she knew that Lenny Dawson would crouch in his hiding-space without the semblance of a sound; all she could do now was to hope that at any rate on this visit he wasn't spotted. The Law would come back, of course; but if it could be fooled on this occasion it might be possible to get Lenny away during the night.

She was interrupted in her thoughts by the girl saying, 'Sorry about all this; it's all a bit of a ghastly imposition, I'm afraid.'

Fenella was feeling slightly apologetic, as most ordinary citizens do when they actually see the Law at work.

Betty turned and looked at her.

'How do you come into it?' she asked, without much real interest.

'I'm with Mr Hefferman, Hooky.'

'Is that what they call him?'

'It's a sort of nickname, because of that nose of his, I suppose. He was looking after Simon Loeson so he's interested, of course.'

'Are you his girl friend?'

'I—' Fenella actually blushed slightly and felt annoyed with herself for doing so. 'Yes, I suppose I am in a way. I didn't exactly want to get mixed up in all this.'

'Well, why don't you keep out of it, then?' the woman said bitterly. 'There's quite enough trouble in the world without stirring up any more. Or perhaps you haven't discovered that yet. Marry him and find out.'

Up in the loft Hooky stood beside Sergeant East and the two men waited for a few moments whilst their eyes grew accustomed to the dim light. There were some bales of hay; an old-fashioned travelling-trunk with a domed lid; the wheel of a cycle and various bits and pieces of domestic debris lying about. Some loops of binder twine hung from a nail on the end wall. It was not a big space and the Sergeant's keen eyes worked slowly round it, missing nothing. Eventually he lifted up the domed top of the travelling-trunk and peered inside. He saw a lady's straw hat; half a dozen sad-looking books, long unread and uncared for by anybody; a brass candlestick and an antiquated typewriter.

'Put that lot in a shop window in The Lanes at Bright, label them "Victoriana" and some fool would pay you good money for them,' Hooky said.

The Sergeant thought it quite likely; in his experience some people were foolish enough to do almost anything.

'I don't actually spot a white Norton motor-cycle,' Hooky said. 'Can you?'

'Not up here,' Sergeant East admitted. 'No, I can't.'

When the two men were once more down in the stable the woman greeted them with 'What *is* up there actually? It's so long since I had a look I've forgotten.'

'It's hellish dark and smells of cheese,' Hooky said. Sergeant East didn't know his Surtees but he thought the description reasonably apt. For a brief moment he even smiled.

'No escaped prisoners or motor-cycles?' Betty asked.

'Perhaps I could have a look in the house,' the Sergeant suggested.

'If you feel you must.'

'I should be more satisfied if I did.'

'I am not really interested in whether you feel satisfied or not, Sergeant. I am interested in getting this ridiculous business cleared up. You must surely be beginning to realize by now that this silly boy has been repaying our kindness to him by inventing a nonsensical story which seems to have fooled the police force completely.'

'Lots of people tell us lies—that's true enough,' the Sergeant agreed, 'so we just have to do our best to sort things out, which are true and which aren't.'

The woman led the way towards the house. At the door she turned and said, 'Do these others have to come with you? I really don't see why I should have to throw the house open to the public.'

'We'll wait outside,' Fenella said with decision.

The Sergeant entered every room in the house including the bathroom and the two loos. If there was a cupboard anywhere he opened the door and peered inside. He got his uniform extremely dusty by taking a good look round in the loft which fulfilled the Surtees quotation even more convincingly than the stable loft had done. The woman accompanied him and said nothing beyond 'This is our bedroom', 'This is the bathroom' and so on.

Outside Hooky and Fenella filled in the time by walking slowly round the stable block together.

'What did you and Mrs Berry talk about whilst we were up in the loft?' Hooky asked.

Fenella laughed. 'You.'

'Me?'

'And other things. The perils of matrimony amongst them. Hooky, I'm not enjoying all this very much.'

'As soon as the Law has finished with us we'll clear off to the Huntsman and, as the immortal Wodehouse says, "Restore the tissues".'

'I've never been able to raise even the beginnings of a smile at Wodehouse. I don't believe any woman can; it's only men who like him.'

'Men are unwise and curiously planned,' Hooky pointed out.

'There aren't any men really. Just overgrown schoolboys. No wonder we have wars and things.'

Hooky did not seem to be in the mood for philosophy.

'It was mighty dark up in that loft,' he said reflectively.

'What do you expect in a loft?' Fenella asked. 'Chandeliers?'

Hooky looked curiously unconvinced by the answer.

Sergeant East and the woman came out of the house and she demanded sarcastically, 'What would you like to search now? The contents of my handbag?'

'I'm only doing my duty, Mrs Baillie-Wilson; and, to put it mildly, you behaved very unwisely in regard to the boy.'

'We did nothing of the sort,' Betty answered with a sudden show of spirit. 'He turned up here lost and I don't say concussed, but certainly shaken and we took him in and looked after him. When he told us he was unhappy at Sheepsgate and didn't want to go back there we said O.K. you can stay here. I don't see that that was being unkind or unwise; and now he's repaying us by making up this ridiculous James Bond story out of something he heard on the radio.'

'I'll let the Super know everything you've said,' the Sergeant promised, and he nodded to Hooky to indicate that they should make their way to the police car. When they were half way there Hooky said casually, 'Let's take a turn round the outside of the stables, shall we?'

The casualness of his tone did not deceive the Sergeant.

'What for?' he asked. 'What's up?'

'I want to ask your opinion of something,' Hooky said blandly. 'May mean nothing, might mean a lot; interesting anyway.'

The two women stood together by the back door of the house watching them.

'I can't think what they're doing now,' Fenella said and Betty answered her bitterly. 'I wish to God you would all clear off, the lot of you, and leave me alone.'

When they turned the corner of the stable building Hooky said, 'Take a squint up at the gable end.'

Without being precisely clear what a gable end was the Sergeant looked up at the end wall of the building.

'Dark in that loft, wasn't it?' Hooky asked.

The Sergeant agreed that it had been confoundedly dark.

'But ought it to have been so dark,' Hooky persisted, 'with three bricks knocked out of the wall?'

Sergeant East scanned the end wall again with renewed interest. There were three gaps in it where bricks had undoubtedly been knocked out. He conjured up a mental picture of what the end wall of the loft had looked like from the inside when he was up there and he couldn't remember three holes through which air and light had come. He lowered his gaze slowly and looked at Hooky.

'Well, that's funny,' he said.

'I said you would find it interesting. Worth another look, wouldn't you say?'

'Definitely,' Sergeant East agreed, 'definitely worth another look.'

'Again?' the woman took up the Sergeant's request; and, just when she was beginning to hope, a band of fear suddenly contracted once more round her heart. 'You want to go up in the loft again? Whatever for?'

'Just to have a look.'

'But you've looked once.'

'If you haven't any objection, Mrs Baillie-Wilson.'

'Well, of course I haven't any objection. There's nothing to see, so why should I have an objection? I just want you to be finished and off the premises, that's all. I'm sick and tired of it.'

'It won't be more than a few minutes,' the Sergeant promised her. 'Just a final look round'; but he thought it might be something more, when she had said that 'Again?' There had been fear in her voice and fear, too, in her eyes; instinct told the Sergeant that he was on to something.

He went into the stable again and was on the point of going up the vertical wall-ladder when he thought of something; he turned away from the ladder and with measured strides paced the full length of the stable. He made it eight yards exactly. He mounted the ladder into the gloomy loft above and with the same slightly exaggerated strides measured that seven paces brought him flush up against the end wall. 'Seven from eight is one,' Sergeant East told himself, and he looked with excited interest at that end wall. It was not made of brick, nor were there three apertures in it conveniently letting in light and air.

The Sergeant moved some odds and ends lying against the wall to one side; he lifted a loop of binder twine from the nail it was hanging on; he began to explore the wall carefully with his two hands.

Suddenly a portion of it moved under his probing fingers and Sergeant East said, 'A-ah.' He lifted the plywood panel out and put it to one side. He peered into the recess he had revealed and saw a face with whose features every policeman in the West Country had been made familiar. The two men stared at one another.

'Lenny Dawson,' Sergeant East said at last and there was a note of triumph in his voice. 'Well, you didn't get far, then, after all, did you?'

Lenny Dawson said nothing; he was thinking of the twenty-five years that lay ahead of him.

SIXTEEN

'ANOTHER CUP, HOOKY?' Miss LeFance asked.

Hooky politely declined. He had come up to the top floor of the house in Gerrard Mews because he felt the urgent necessity of talking to someone, not because he wanted a cup of Gloria LeFance's tea. Gloria's tea was even worse than her coffee and in Hooky's opinion no sane man would deliberately go in search of it, but when he came into the room Gloria's kettle was boiling and there was no escape. Without rudeness he could hardly refuse; but enough was enough and he felt entitled to say 'no' to the offer of a second cup.

Such a defeatist attitude did not much appeal to Miss LeFance; she poured herself out a second cup of the villainously strong liquid as, in due course, she would pour out a third and fourth one.

Hooky studied her as she was doing it. Life had never been over-kind to her and she was beginning to show signs of the struggle. The yellow of the hair was not very convincing, the face looked thin and strained beneath the make-up. The make-up itself had not been applied quite as carefully as it used to be. Perhaps she doesn't mind much now, Hooky thought.

'Did you enjoy your holiday?' Miss LeFance asked.

'It had its moments.'

'Were you doing some sort of a job?'

'In a way. Incidentally I got the sack.'

'You got the sack, Hooky? Who dare do a thing like that?'

Hooky laughed at the implied compliment.

'A man with a lot of money,' he said. 'But fair dos; from his point of view he was quite justified. I was sacked for neglect of duty. I should have been looking after the rich man's son; but, alas, actually I was looking after another man's daughter.'

Miss LeFance smiled; this was more like the Hooky she knew; she liked him to be in character. She reached for his cup.

'You had better let me read the leaves. Maybe I can see something nice in them for you.'

Miss LeFance, on whom Fortune had smiled but seldom in life, was a great one for signs and portents—a person's hand, tealeaves in a cup, the Tarot cards were all consulted in turn and all meant a lot to her.

Hooky was well acquainted with her superstitions and occasionally took advantage of them, half-scoffing, half-believing; but this time he denied her and refused to hand his teacup across. He wasn't much interested in what Gloria LeFance might allege the tealeaves to say; he was desperately interested in what Fenella was going to say (he took a quick look at his wristwatch) almost any minute now.

'I've got a visitor coming in a few minutes,' he said.

Gloria looked at him. 'A girl?'

'A girl.'

'The girl you were with when you ought to have been doing something else?'

'The very same.'

'Hooky—is she *the* girl?'

H. E. R. Hefferman had been about a bit; he had shot his man and begot his man; he had had his illusions and disillusions; he had lived. And now the oldest, divinest idiocy of all had settled on him. He nodded. 'Yes, she's the girl,' he said. 'The one and only.'

'Hooky, how marvellous!'

'If she says "yes".'

'You haven't asked her yet?'

'I'm going to shortly.'

'Hooky, I *must* look in your cup.'

'No, don't, for God's sake; it might say she isn't going to have me.'

'Hooky, it couldn't.'

'You're an incurable romantic, Gloria.'

'Who wants to be cured of romance?'

'Not I. No, indeed, not I. Not now. But Fenella's young, she's lovely, she's all the bright things you ever dreamed about; she's the sunshine coming in through the open window on a spring day; and I'm not any of those things, Gloria. Let's face it; I'm not any of those things. A man lives and knocks about and thinks he's clever to give life a buffet or two; but every time he does Life gets its own back; it leaves a mark on him. And there are plenty of marks on me. So why should she say "yes"?'

'As you won't let me read your cup I can't tell you if she will say "yes",' Gloria said, 'but I can tell you *why* she should. If she's got any sense she'll say "yes" because you're a kind man, Hooky; you're good; not goody-good—God knows you aren't that; but you're decent; you give your word and you stick to it; you'll make any woman a splendid mate; you're genuine.'

Hooky was slightly overwhelmed by this tribute to his virtues and for the moment was at a loss as to how to reply to it. Whilst he was hesitating the door opened and Roly Watkins, the factotum of the establishment looked in.

'Sorry to interrupt your *tate-ar*, miss,' he said, 'but 'is nibs is wanted downstairs.'

For a moment there was silence; Gloria LeFance was watching Hooky, fascinated. Hooky was telling himself not to be in such a funk—for that was the truth of it; he was in a blue funk. Fenella might not say 'yes'; at that moment it seemed extremely unlikely to him that she would say 'yes'.

'Who is it who wants me?' he asked.

Roly grinned his lascivious grin.

'A young lady, Mr H. The one 'oo came 'ere once before. The good looker. The one as *is* a lady. The goods.'

FENELLA, HER EYES DANCING with amused affection, remarked what a lovely day it was.

Grasping gratefully at any straw of normal conversation, Hooky agreed.

There was a cold wind, Fenella pointed out, a deceptive treacherous little north-east wind, but the sunshine was lovely. Hooky said that even dingy, dirty, drab old Soho cheered up a bit when the sun shone on it.

An awkward silence fell on the room; of the two people there Fenella was conspicuously the more at ease.

She broke the silence by asking gently, 'Hooky, when you invited me round here was it in order to ask me to marry you?'

'That was on the agenda,' Hooky admitted, slightly taken aback by the directness of the question.

'I need hardly say that I feel complimented.'

'Why even should you feel that? It's a pretty lunatic proposition from your point of view. I am suggesting that you ally yourself with a man considerably older than you are; whose bank balance is virtually non-existent; whose income is extremely doubtful; whose character is reprehensible and whose one remaining relative, an aunt, is extremely formidable.'

Fenella smiled at him. 'Oh, Hooky, those things don't matter much; in fact, some of them are rather nice; but—oh dear, it isn't easy to say this, yet it has to be said—I don't believe it would work, Hooky; I don't believe you are a marrying animal.'

'Damn it all, Fen,' Hooky answered with some heat. 'I know whether I want to get married or not.'

'Are you sure you do? Think it over, Hooky. Will you still want it in a year's time?'

'How the devil do I know what I shall want in a year's time?' Hooky roared.

Fenella threw her shapely young head back and laughed loud and long.

'You're on probation for a year, Hooky,' she announced. 'If you feel the same at the end of twelve months maybe we'll do a deal. Meanwhile I'm doing nothing this evening for dinner.'

'Wrong again. You're having dinner with me.'

'Thank you kindly, sir,' she said.

'Three hundred and sixty-five days,' Hooky said. 'Well, thank God it isn't a leap year. I'll mark them off every night on a calendar.'

"A most impressive debut—witty, warm and well conceived."
—*The Patriot Ledger*

Murder in Mendocino

MARY KITTREDGE

Abdicating as queen of the home-repair guides, author Charlotte Kent fled to quaint Pelican Rock to produce a "real" book; the biography of the California town's most famous—and tragic—historical figure, Dr. Stanley Hardwicke.

Then one of her creative-writing students smugly flaunts her own imminent success on the same subject. However, obnoxious Rena Blount is fatally shot before Charlotte can throttle her.

Was Rena murdered because of what she knew—or what the killer thought she knew—about Hardwicke? Pelican Rock's older citizens are strangely silent about the mysterious doctor...and now a teenage boy has disappeared. Is there a connection? Charlotte starts digging—and discovers the past may die...but murder lives on.

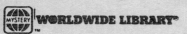

"Nothing is more satisfying than a mystery concocted by one of the pros." —*L.A. Times*

Hugh Pentecost
Winner of the Mystery Writers of America Award